PRAISE FOR ANNE LANGE

For *Friends with Benefits*

"What a nice ménage romance! All three main characters were lovable. I definitely recommend it."　　*—Mary's Ménage Whispers*

"The best part about this book? It also has a real story going on in between the sex scenes. Friends with Benefits is emotional, heartwarming, anger evoking, thought provoking, passionate and sigh worthy."　　　　　　　　*—Robin, Book Reads and Reviews*

For *Hers to Own*

"I really enjoyed reading this book, it was fun and had some thrill. It's not your typical romance story which is why I think it works. It not only deals with BDSM but body image and what you can do to get over a bad body image and tell yourself not only are you beautiful but believe it as well. I recommend this book with immense pleasure."　　*—Wild Rayne Night Owl Reviews Top Pick – 4.5 Stars*

"I really enjoyed this book and the characters! Sexy story with a great message, would definitely recommend!"
　　　　　　　　—Casey Ramblings From This Chick – 4 Stars

For *Wicked Indulgence*

"A great read! I couldn't get enough! The story line sucks you in and shows you the crazy twists, turns, the sexy fun, the bad, the good and the really really really good!

"A ménage story that gives you love, emotions and things that need forgiving! Jamie is hot, sexy Dom that came from not having much money! But was in love with a beautiful girl who did come from money! One night and her father changes both their lives!"

—Maria York ~ *Book Boyfriend Hangover* – 5 Stars

"Anne Lange is an author on my follow list and for a good reason. Her books are filled with sensual imagery and it never fails I want to live in the worlds she has created. Her Vault series is just such a place. A club with sexy Doms and succulent submissives who enjoy the feel of a paddle on their skin. […] The sex scenes were smoking hot and push a little toward boundaries. A great read."

—Dana19018 – 4 Stars

For *Sliding into Home*

"Anne Lang hits a homerun with her novella Sliding Into Home about second chances. It's an easy-to-read story, full of self-exploration and emotion. A set-up between friends is the catalyst with Las Vegas the setting for a fun tale of life changes and the decisions they bring. Character development is good as both Jack and Devyn have a history both with each other and without to contend with."

—*Tangled Hearts Book Reviews* – 4 Stars

"This was a great fast read. The characters were great, they were funny, sexy. Their interactions were smooth and the story flowed very well. Jack and Devyn re-find each other with the help of their meddling friends. The spark is certainly still there after all this time as well as the deeply hidden love they once shared. Jack needs something to save him from himself and Devyn may be the one to open his eyes to it. It was fun to read about their wild night in Vegas and the morning after. This was a great book to curl up with. It didn't have a lot of drama, but plenty of steam as well as re-finding lost love."

—*The Book Quarry* – 4 Stars

For *The Final Quarter*

"The beginning of the story leaves wondering how this book will end. By the end of the first chapter, I excited to see how this book will turn out. The author did a good job of drawing the reader into the world she created. The world is very realistic and the author established a sense of time and location to help the reader created a picture of what the world would look like. The pace of the story was a bit slow at some points and fast is others. The main characters and the secondary characters were fascinating and believable. I loved that no matter how tough things got Serena stood by Mitch. While Mitch has many faults he handled them in a realistic and believable way. [...] I hope we get to see these characters again in the future. I can't wait to read the next book in the series."

—*Night Owl Reviews* – 4.5 Stars

"After exchanging vows, a couple is expected to live happily ever after. In THE FINAL QUARTER by Anne Lange, the second book in A New League Series, focuses on what happens when communication gets lost in a marriage. [...]

"Although I wanted to jump right into a resolution for the couple, as a reader I knew I was in for some angst. That's where the title comes into play. It's the final quarter of their marriage and the clock is counting down. The heat level provides a solid addition to the storyline, giving the couple just the right amount of intensity."

—*The Romance Reviews* – 4 Stars

OTHER TITLES BY ANNE LANGE

THE VAULT SERIES
FRIENDS WITH BENEFITS
THE PERFECT MOMENT
HERS TO OWN
WICKED INDULGENCE
WHO'S THE BOSS?

A NEW LEAGUE SERIES
SLIDING INTO HOME
THE FINAL QUARTER

FAMILY TIES SERIES
HER CHOICE

SHORT STORIES (15K OR LESS)
WITH THE GREATEST OF EASE
BLIND TASTE TEST
GAME NIGHT

COMING SOON
FOREVER STARTS TODAY

Check out Anne's Website for more information about these books.
http://www.authorannelange.com/

Get your free copy of Game Night
http://dl.bookfunnel.com/eysouov4fz

Worth the Risk

ANNE LANGE

hotRom publishing
OTTAWA, ONTARIO

Editing: Anne Lange

Cover Design: Bookin' It Designs
http://www.bookinitdesigns.com/

Cover Photo Copyright © Kruse Images and Photography
http://www.facebook.com/kipmodelsandboudoir

Models: Lance Jones and Kimberleigh Michelle

Book Layout & Design: Ryan Fitzgerald
http://ryanjamesfitzgerald.ca/

First publication (electronic only) Etopia Press: January 2013

Due to the dynamic nature of the Internet, website links contained within this book may be outdated and/or no longer valid.

AUTHOR'S NOTE

This book was originally published in 2013 by Etopia Press in digital format only.

All rights were transferred back to the author in January of 2016.

This book has been revised and updated to enhance the characters and storyline, but the content has not been significantly altered, meaning the original plot remains intact.

This book is now available in both digital and print formats.

DEDICATION

As I re-read this book in preparation to re-release it, I was swept back in time remembering my joy and astonishment at having my very first book published.

My husband tells me this one is his favorite. It holds a special place in my heart too, because it was written to help heal a painful moment in my life.

My husband was beside me then, just as he's beside me now, all these years later.

Love you. xoxo

A weekend of hot sex can't erase past heartbreaks, but it might lead to a better tomorrow.

Molly arrives at a beautiful park, ready to spend the holiday camping with friends. This weekend is the highlight of her year—or it was, until Tanner Daivies showed up. Her high school crush is all grown up, sexy as sin, and he's demanding answers—answers Molly isn't sure she can give.

Years ago, Molly Simpson broke his heart. When the woman he loved told him she needed space, Tanner gave it to her—for ten long years. Now he's back. He'll settle for closure but hopes for a future. Sex with Molly is scorching hot and brings back plenty of memories. When they're together, it's clear they were never meant to be apart.

It may be time to deal with the past. But is reliving it worth the risk?

Worth the Risk

PROLOGUE

Ten Years Earlier

MOLLY ARCHED HER NECK, LEANING INTO Tanner. She groaned when his mouth latched on to the sensitive spot just south of her earlobe. He knew her so well. Twenty years ago they'd met when their moms joined a "Mommy and Me" playgroup. At the tender age of three, they'd squared off over a box filled with Tonka trucks. Now he traveled paths along her skin rather than in granules of sand.

"I'm ready for dessert." His breath whispered across her ear. "Let's head to bed."

"Ice cream in bed?"

"No, you in bed."

Her gaze dropped to the long, hard ridge straining against the fly of his jeans. Curving her lips, she created the semblance of a grin. "Aren't you ever at rest?"

"Hey, I'm a normal guy who has a very sexy girlfriend. Other than getting through finals and graduation, sex is the usual thing on my mind, especially when I have the pleasure of coming home to you." He traversed a finger down her arm, scraped a blunt nail across the delicate skin at her wrist, and entwined his hand with hers. "Come on. I want to show you just how much I love you." He stood, plucking her from the sofa with enough force she stumbled, crashing against his broad chest. She had to tilt her neck back to see his face. His eyes darkened with lust as he brushed his lips against hers.

1

"I want to eat you up, fuck you silly, and then start all over again."

He spun on his heel, towing her behind him. She curled her toes into the carpet, firming her resolve, searching for purchase every few feet. And then she glanced at him, pictured her future, and caved. Defeated, she followed him down the short hallway to their small bedroom, throat aching from some unnamed emotion. No, she knew—guilt.

Each day the situation became more difficult for her to cope with. Her heart thumped, skipping a beat or maybe two. She raised her left hand to her right breast. Could he hear it?

He reached the side of their bed and turned to face her, raising his hands to cup her face, his large fingers playing with the hair at the base of her neck.

She tried to peel her gaze away from the man looking at her with such devotion, swallowing over that lump of self-remorse lodged in between her heart and tonsils.

He frowned down at her. "Hey, you okay?"

"Yeah, sure. Um…just hard to believe we'll be university graduates in a few short weeks."

"Forget about that for now." He released her and reached down to grab the hem of her shirt. One tug and he wrenched it up and over her head. "I love when you don't wear a bra." He grinned like the horn dog he was. "Saves time." He bent down and grasped one nipple in his warm mouth, sucking hard. Would anybody ever be as impatient and enthusiastic to have her as Tanner?

She closed her eyes and swallowed past that lump of emotion. One last time—that's what this was—one last time.

Returning his hands to her waist, Tanner switched his attention to her other breast. His teeth encircled the tender nub, his tongue swiping the end, driving her crazy. In a flick, the button on her pants came undone, and he lowered the zipper.

He pushed her jeans and panties down over her hips, shoving until they puddled around her ankles. "Step out."

She did, gazing straight ahead, looking out the window to the duck pond in the park across the road. From their fifth floor apartment, all she could make out were bodies on the walking path—joggers, couples...and families.

She sucked in her breath, closing her eyes to block the image.

A throaty moan jerked her concentration back to the man worshiping her body. He whirled her around, walking her two steps backward until she plopped down on the bed. With one hand on her chest, he tipped her back, and with the other, he nudged her legs apart. Then he fell to his knees, and his mouth latched on to her next favorite spot.

"Mmm...I can't decide. Vanilla? Chocolate?" His hands held her thighs wide, his tongue lapped along her moist slit and then circled her clit twice before flicking the little bud a few times. "Or maybe cherry? Oh, yes, definitely cherry."

She wanted to giggle at his silliness, any other time she would, but not today. Today she couldn't find the humor.

He made a feast of her, ramping her up, easing off, and starting again.

She twisted her body and writhed under his hands. She elevated her hips, pushing her pussy against his face.

3

He reached up and tugged on her nipples, tweaking them into hard, excited points. He caressed her legs and inner thighs until she squirmed on the bed, so close to begging for release.

It seemed an eternity passed. Then he stroked two fingers along the slippery smooth skin before teasing her with a shallow dip and finally plunging deep inside. He pumped in and out.

Those thick digits filled her, but still, she wanted more. She needed more. She worked her hips, keeping time with each thrust. Almost there.

His fingers moved, tunneling faster, harder. He sucked on her clit, but it wasn't enough.

"Make me come."

Her gasped plea brought forth a deep chuckle. "Your wish is my command, baby."

"What?" She paused, her brain choosing that moment to zero in on his innocent choice of words.

"Come for me, baby."

She froze. That quick, the climax that had been spiraling out of control fizzled and sputtered out. She collapsed against the bed and swallowed back an anguished cry, biting her lip hard in the process. "Stop." She pushed him away when he reached for her and sat up, struggling to back up against the headboard.

"Molly, what's wrong?" He remained on his knees at the side of the bed, confusion marring his handsome face.

She squeezed her eyes tight and sighed. When she opened them, his face shimmered out of focus. "Tanner—" She licked her dry lips to try again.

He waited.

Her heart cracked wide open. God help her, she couldn't do this to him? Words fell from her mouth, stumbling over each other in her haste to spit them out.

But it wasn't the words she'd practiced.

Tanner loved her. He'd want to take care of her. She refused to destroy his plans when he could do nothing anyway. "I can't do this anymore. I think we should split up."

His head lurched back, and an odd sound exploded from his throat. "What? Is this a joke?"

"No. It's no joke. I'm sorry." She grabbed the comforter, wrapping it tight around her body, right up to just under her chin. Distance. She needed distance.

"I'm confused, Molly. Everything's been good. We're graduating; we're ready to begin our lives. What do you mean you can't do this anymore? For Christ's sake, we've been together forever."

"I—"

He jumped to his feet and marched a few steps away. He stopped, spinning to stare at her, his mouth hanging open as he swept his arm back and forth between them. His words, when they came, filled her with anguish. "What the hell was this? A good-bye fuck?"

She flinched at the harshness in his voice. "I've been thinking a lot lately," she tried. She hated this. But thought it best, for Tanner. He had such a bright future. "I've never been on my own. I need to be on my own for a little while." Cold seeped into her fingers and toes. Tiny shivers racked her body. Molly held tighter to the blanket, willing her teeth not to chatter, not to stutter over the words she struggled to say. "We've never dated anybody else Tanner. Maybe—"

"Maybe what?" he demanded, his eyes a mix of anger and deep hurt.

"She gulped over the lie lodged in her throat. "I believe we owe it to ourselves to explore our options." Inwardly she winced. What a grown-up piece of crap.

"Explore our options? What kind of options do you want to explore? Wait. Is there another guy?"

"No! I—"

"I thought you loved me, Molly. I thought we had plans for a future—together." He shifted toward her, reaching out again, but she shook her head. He dropped his hand. He sucked in two shuddering breaths and spun away from her. He made it as far as the door and stopped. With one hand on the knob, his back to her, his shoulders hunched forward. "I can't change your mind?"

The pain in his voice almost made her say yes. *Almost.*

"This is really what you want?" he asked.

"Yes." She dipped her chin to the comforter, muffling her response.

"But—"

She raised her head. "Yes." She bit into her lower lip again, tasting copper, unable to hold back the dam as it spilled over and rolled down her cheeks.

He opened the door.

"Tanner—"

He stilled, his back rigid.

"I'm so sorry. I hope someday you'll be able to forgive me."

He cast a quick glance over his shoulder, his face etched with hurt, his eyes blazing with fury now. Then he left their bedroom, closing the door behind him with a soft click.

When the door to the spare room slammed closed, she flinched.

Molly grabbed a pillow and clutched it to her chest, her knees tucked up tight under her. She couldn't see through the tears. She fell to her side and curled into a tighter ball, her hands fisting the blankets, and cried harder.

The morning sun filtering through the blinds on the window woke her. God, what a horrible night. She ached everywhere.

Molly rubbed at her dry, puffy eyes. She couldn't recall succumbing to exhaustion. But she did remember that at some point during her melt down she realized she'd made a horrible mistake, and promised to rectify it in the morning

Scrambling off the bed, she tiptoed to the bedroom door and laid her ear against it, holding her breath. Only the ticking of the kitchen clock broke the silence. How in heavens would she face him this morning? He'd be angry, probably as hurt as she'd been. As she still was, but he'd understand. She'd make him understand.

Molly opened the door and stepped into the hall. As she inched down the hallway, the silence of an empty apartment engulfed her. When she reached the kitchen, she ignored the dirty dishes, the pizza box and the stack of restaurant brochures Tanner had been pouring over as he talked with such enthusiasm about how one day he'd have his own place.

Instead, her gaze zeroed in on the table, where in the very center lay a lone silver key.

She stepped over the cold tile floor, her foot nudging one of her slippers she'd kicked off her feet last night while they'd eaten pizza and talked about their upcoming graduation ceremony.

Molly reached out and picked up the key, her fingers trembling. The metal chilled her hand.

A solitary tear slid down her check.

Tanner was gone.

CHAPTER ONE

Present Day

O H. MY. GOD. SHE STUMBLED BACKWARD, HIT A chair, and plopped into the canvas seat. The chair tipped, but she grabbed the arms and wrestled it down into place. Holy shit. Did he recognize her? Crap. She didn't need this. Not now. Molly dropped her head into her hands, hiding her face. What the hell was Tanner Daivies doing there?

Shrieks filled the air as her friends spotted and recognized him. While they ran over to greet their long-lost friend, Molly rose from the chair. Moving around behind it, she stepped back a few paces and stumbled. Somebody reached out and saved from falling on her ass Molly peered into her best friend's surprised face. Colleen's sweet, open personality typically drew people in, encouraging most to confess their sins or fall at her feet and do her bidding. But not Molly—and not for lack of trying on her friend's part. Molly guarded her secrets like a mama bear. And for a good reason—guilt—a power motivator.

Knowing her own smile wobbled, she opened her mouth to make light of her clumsiness, but nothing came out. From the corner of her eye, she spotted Colleen's current boyfriend, Steve, grinning like a fool, heading into the fray. This new addition would no doubt cause Tanner to question his memory of their cluster of friends. He didn't need to worry—nobody had met Steve prior to this weekend. Her friend changed boyfriends as often as she changed handbags.

Colleen grasped Molly's shoulders and leaned in close, her voice dropping low. "Are you okay?"

It was really him. Curiosity got the better of her, and she glanced back over her shoulder. Memories assaulted her as he removed his six-foot-plus frame from the car to stand in the center of the welcome circle. Her friends were all talking at him, their voices filled with excitement. Judging by his glazed expression, their reaction left him a little overwhelmed.

Ten years. She rubbed her chest, thinking back to the invisible ache that had bothered her earlier on the drive here. She'd struggled the entire two hours to keep her focus on the road and not on painful memories from the past.

She flexed her fingers. Maybe the cause of her earlier distress was the fact that this year served as a milestone. Ten years since graduation, ten years since she last saw Tanner, and ten years since…*fuck.* When did she start counting? Molly searched the area for possible escape routes.

Colleen's gentle shake brought her back to the moment. "Brad texted me earlier and said he took the afternoon off. He also said he was bringing a surprise with him. He's been dating somebody new. I just assumed—"

"Um…yeah. I wouldn't have expected Brad's surprise to be Tanner either. It…ah…caught me off guard. That's—" *Oh, crap.* "I just need a few minutes."

"You've got no color in your face."

Molly's heart palpitated. Colleen's mouth moved, but the buzz in her ears drowned out the words. She swallowed hard. Air, she needed air.

"I'm sure it might be awkward, but, the others won't let him cause a scene. You're the one we've stayed close to over the years, not him. Our allegiance is to you, honey."

Molly swung her gaze to where her childhood friends had gathered around the car, effectively pinning Tanner against it. She wasn't so sure about that. Sam and Olivia, a couple since they were in diapers and married now, both glowed like beacons. Violet, a transplant from Toronto when her parents divorced, hovered close, waiting for her turn to say hi to an old friend.

Brad and Tanner had been best friends through grade school and high school. Brad had been pissed when Tanner left town without a word to anyone. Looked as though he got over it.

They'd all asked. But Molly had never told anybody why she and Tanner broke up. She'd stressed over it at the time, deflecting comments from friends about him disappearing days before graduation. She hated the thought of being subjected to the pity she'd see on their faces if they knew the truth. Everybody assumed the breakup had been his doing. She never corrected them.

Colleen's words began to cut through the insistent noise.

Molly nodded. "Thank you. That means more to me than you know." Unshed tears burned her eyes. She opened her mouth and sucked in a shaky breath, but at least she had oxygen in her lungs now. "You're right. It will be…fine." She gulped. "Why don't you go over and say hi?"

"Are you sure?"

"Yeah. I'm going to wait here for a few more minutes." She

began calculating the odds of sneaking past her friends and making a quick getaway before any of them noticed.

Colleen gave her arm a final squeeze and walked over to join the others.

Breathe in. Breathe out. Molly closed her eyes, wishing for a paper bag. A really big one. She so did not need this in her life right now.

* * *

His friends charged toward him, grinning wide, excitement in their voices, happiness in their eyes, the girls squealing. Tanner's mind jumped back to a time when they were young, gangly teenagers. Thinner versions of what faced him today, with longer hair, and carefree attitudes ready to take on the world. In some ways, it seemed no time had passed. In others, a lifetime.

When he'd run into Brad while getting beer in town, Tanner had tried to wiggle out of the invitation to reunite with his old friends for their annual camping trip. Being reminded of what he'd missed out on over the last decade didn't sit well. But the enticement of seeing his old friends overrode his misgivings.

After apologizing to his parents for yet another sudden departure, he joined Brad on a drive around town, taking in the sights, sounds, and smells of spring in a small town—nothing had changed.

Unable to speak through the noisy assault, he struggled just to stay standing, shaking hands with a guy he didn't know while the girls hung from his shoulders. Their exuberant welcome humbled him. He'd run out of their lives without a word to anyone. Not his best friend, not his ex-girlfriend, barely his parents. And in all the years in between, he never reached out, not once.

As he greeted them, his gaze kept straying to the one person he both needed and feared to see. When Brad first drove into the campsite, Tanner had feigned dropping something to avoid looking for her. No such luck. Whatever mechanism in his body or his brain that ruled him—maybe it was his dick— forced his eyes to seek her out. Like a missile detecting her heat, his gaze zeroed in on the target—Molly Simpson. Then his heart tripped, it actually seemed to skip a beat, startled by the impact of seeing her again. No mistaking the fact that she recognized him. Her eyes had widened, the blood drained from her face, and her mouth dropped open in obvious shock before she stumbled into a chair.

Now, she stood by the fire, angled away from him, sneaking furtive glances in his direction. The stiff way she held herself betrayed her attempt at nonchalance. He could almost hear the questions racing through her head.

Damn, she was beautiful. The grown-up Molly stole his breath. Ash-blonde hair, cut in a fashionable style, fell in gentle waves around her shoulders. Standing in a campground, surrounded by trees, even dressed in shorts, a T-shirt, and runners, she projected an impression of understated sophistication. It was as natural to her as breathing.

She stood a solid eight to ten inches shorter than him. He remembered teasing her about her height every time he bent down to kiss her. God, he missed kissing her. He curved his lips into a smile as his gaze wandered over the rest of her. Still slender and toned, she had the strength of an athlete and the grace of a dancer. He had been so hot for her back then, certain their love would last forever.

He didn't know if anyone knew why he and Molly had broken up. Hell, *he* didn't even know why it happened. One minute they were getting ready to graduate from university and start their lives together and the next she was telling him she wanted to be on her own. Well, he'd granted her wish. He'd left without saying good-bye and hadn't seen her or any of the rest of his family or friends since. Nobody understood how much her rejection had hurt him back then.

Nor was he ready to admit the real reason he'd come back home now.

He shook his head to dislodge the memory. In the past, every time he'd thought about that day, his blood would boil. But now the anger wouldn't come. In its place, he discovered disappointment and something else…resignation maybe? What changed? Over the years he'd had relationships with other women, though not one of them evolved beyond casual dating.

Maybe time had simply worked its magic. His hurt outweighed the anger now. He also still had—and suspected he would always have—feelings for her.

Did she think about him? Feel anything for him? For all he knew she was happy, married, with a couple of kids. She deserved that. He tried to ignore the knot in his stomach. But even after all these years, the mere idea of another man's child growing in her belly pissed him off.

Damn it. He was entitled to answers. If she had moved on, fine, he would be gracious and back away—he hadn't come home to interfere. But, if she hadn't, then perhaps a possibility existed for them to…what? To be friends? To start over?

"I can't believe it's you, man. It's great to see you." Sam's deep voice penetrated his thoughts.

Tanner reached out to shake his hand, while he enticed Olivia to step closer for a hug. "Look at you two. I heard you finally got married. Sorry I couldn't make it back for the wedding. My parents said you looked stunning, Liv."

The petit brunette blushed, sidled next to her husband, and circled his waist with her arm. "Not to worry; we have lots of pictures. Are you in town for a while?"

"I'm—"

"Hey, guys." Brad smiled at the crowd. "Why don't we let the man step away from the car? Help us get our tent pitched, and then we'll let him fill us in on what he's been up to over a beer. I don't know about the rest of you, but it's been a long week for me and I'd love to sit down, put my feet up, and get this long weekend started."

Thankful for the slight reprieve, Tanner helped Brad unload the gear. Soon enough, he'd have to face the inquisition from his friends.

Soon enough Molly would face his.

CHAPTER TWO

*T*EN YEARS. MOLLY STOOD ROOTED TO THE GROUND as her friends welcomed Tanner back, looking away each time his glance clashed with hers. Should she stay, get it over with, or run and hide? Was he home to stay or was this simply a visit? She knew his parents didn't see him as often as they'd like. He'd fled to Vancouver, and as far as she knew, he'd never been back, forcing them to travel west to see their son.

Tanner had left their apartment late that night and never returned. He didn't even show up for graduation.

Molly had stayed in Ottawa. She enjoyed living in the city, and she loved her job as a magazine editor. She excelled at it, and had friends there. However, these trips were the highlight of her existence. Each year, she needed to reconnect with the people who really understood her. After losing her parents, this annual get together grounded her.

The crunch of gravel drew her gaze. A dark blue SUV rolled in behind her red Mazda. The last of the bunch, Matt, picked the perfect moment to arrive. However, the placement of his car created an effective barrier. She wasn't going anywhere now.

He climbed from his car and retrieved something from the back. Colleen jogged over to help him. Desperate for a distraction, Molly dragged her attention from Tanner and, through sheer force of will, switched it to Colleen and Matt. They rummaged around for a couple minutes in the back of his car and then backed out with three trays of coffees and two boxes of donuts.

Caffeine and sugar. That should make her feel better. A beer would work faster.

She kept a speculative eye on Tanner through lowered lashes. Time passed in a haze of memories. When Tanner extricated himself from the group and sauntered toward her, she jerked back to the present, straightening her spine and standing.

He studied her, his head cocked slightly to the right. He approached as though he expected her to flee. With each step that brought him closer, her heartbeat picked up and her nipples hardened until they peaked to stiff points beneath her shirt.

Molly crossed her arms over her chest. Warmth unfurled low in her belly. She couldn't do much about her damp panties. It had been a long time, but seemingly, her heart and her body hadn't suffered from memory loss and after a decade of yearning, decided to go for broke.

Tanner stopped five feet away and then closed the distance by three. She'd forgotten how tall he was. His dark hair grazed his shoulders in a shaggy, but masculine mess. The years had been kind to him. Her mouth watered for the second time today. And again, some oxygen would be nice.

He wore a pair of chocolate brown boots, well-worn jeans, and a body-hugging black T-shirt made with his specific measurements in mind. It outlined every muscle he had, and he had plenty. She pressed her lips together, tight. No need to embarrass herself by drooling.

"Hello, Molly." His voice was deeper, his face leaner, and though he'd dropped his shades over his eyes to block the glare of the setting sun when he got out of the car, she remembered their swirling gray depths. Regardless of his mood, looking into his eyes always made her picture an overcast day, the clouds heavy with the promise of rain.

"Tanner."

The sounds of her friends talking, other campers arriving and setting up, and children playing a game of tag over in the field all became background noise, fading away while they stood, drinking each other in. He had matured. His body, his demeanor, everything about him spoke volumes of the man he had become—a harder version of the young man she had known, of the boy she had loved. He oozed confidence and sensuality.

Her body hummed its approval. Visions of her arms and legs, entangled with his, danced through her head. Good thing she packed extra undies.

Colleen chose that moment to interrupt them, strategically placing herself between their bodies. How her friend managed to avoid getting singed, Molly would never know. "Hey, you two. Grab a drink, or a coffee and a donut, and let's catch up. We're all dying to know what you've been up to, Tanner."

The spell broken, Molly closed her eyes and dropped her head, dragging in a deep gulp of fresh air.

Tanner cleared his throat. "Uh, sure. Brad and I are going to get the tent pitched first."

With Colleen as her shield, Molly kept her eyes to ground, but she could feel Tanner's gaze boring into the top of her head before he excused himself to join the others.

Colleen spun around and grabbed Molly's hand, yanking her over a few steps. "Wow. You two seemed to have forgotten the rest of us were here."

"I didn't know what to say to him. I'm stunned he's here. You're sure you didn't know he was coming?" Surely, her friend wouldn't have kept her in the dark. Had Molly known, she never would have made the trip this year.

"I'm as surprised as you. While you two were staring each other down, I grilled Brad. Apparently, Tanner just got back to town. Brad ran into him this morning and invited him." Colleen frowned, but held Molly's gaze. Her voice a whisper, she asked the same question she'd asked many times over the ages. "What happened between the two of you, Molly? Are you ever going to tell me?"

Colleen had never pushed for an explanation. Molly regretted that she couldn't confide in her best friend, but it had nothing to do with trust and everything to do with grief, guilt, and the pact she'd made with herself. "It was a long time ago, and something I don't think about anymore. I'd prefer to leave it in the past." In truth, it never drifted far from her thoughts. She had worked long and hard to get to the point where she remembered without the constant threat of tears. The guilt still needed work.

She shook her head. Ten years had passed in the blink of an eye. She'd decided long ago to never tell a soul. And with her parents gone, that promise had been easy to keep. She just hoped that somewhere along the way Tanner had forgiven her for ending things the way she had.

Colleen offered her a sympathetic smile and hauled her in close for a hug.

Molly closed her eyes and drew in a deep breath, releasing it on a sigh of relief. She'd been granted another reprieve from divulging her secret, at least for now.

* * *

Brad raised his beer. "Here's to the official start of blackfly season and a long weekend with no rain."

"Are you kidding me?" Matt's hoot of laughter made the others smile. "This is Canada, and it's May Two-Four. That's synonymous with cold, damp, and wet."

Molly couldn't agree more. But like most Canadians, this weekend was a tradition, regardless of the weather. Somewhat comparable to giving birth and forgetting about the pain—something Molly would never experience.

Bottles clinked around the table. After Brad, Tanner, and Matt had finished pitching their tents around the double site and stowed their gear, they gathered around the picnic tables. Molly chose the end opposite Tanner, where she could observe unnoticed.

The remains of sandwiches and a variety of junk food lay scattered among them. A few chipmunks, moving past their stage of shyness, darted in and out grabbing dropped crumbs. The noise level had risen as the other weekend campers arrived. A group of young kids started a game of horseshoes at the site across from them, the ping of steel on steel sporadic throughout the late afternoon.

From beneath lowered lids, she watched Tanner survey the area.

"You managed to snag a perfect spot." He nodded his appreciation.

Sam snatched up a handful of chips. "Me and Liv came in early and booked them for us. Good thing, too, because the park's full. Snagging this end of the loop was lucky."

"So, Tanner, have you been in Vancouver all this time?" Matt asked the question everyone wanted to know.

"Yes, but most of the time I've been up at Whistler. I originally went out to visit my aunt and uncle in Vancouver. Then I got a summer job at the ski hill working in one of the restaurants." Tanner sipped from his beer. "I stayed at the hill for a year, living with friends while I worked." He shrugged. "I had nothing to come home to, so I decided to stay." Molly's gaze jumped to Tanner's, but even without his glasses, his eyes were hooded, his thoughts hidden.

The strained silence seemed to last forever, but it only existed between the two of them. Molly scanned the others around the table until her gaze collided with Colleen's. Molly ducked her head.

"You know, I can still remember our first trip out here," Matt said.

"Yeah, the year we graduated from high school. God, we were just kids." Brad laughed. He grew serious and tossed a pointed stare in Tanner's direction. "You know, over the years I've seen plenty of people leave town. They don't visit too often. In a small town, that hits families hard. We've missed you, man."

"I know. I'm sorry I didn't keep in touch. Nothing's changed much in town though."

"Nothing ever changes around here." Matt took a drink of his beer.

"I noticed old Mrs. Peterson still has her garden of tulips in every color."

"Yeah, but she doesn't have Mr. Peterson to help her care for it anymore. Her daughter comes every fall and plants a few new bulbs to replace any the squirrels dug up, and she comes back to clean it out before end of summer."

"Can't say I've missed the smell of pine trees and spring flowers mixed in with the aroma of discarded cigarette butts, thawing mud, and dog crap being slowly revealed by the melting snow." The guys laughed, but Molly felt certain she detected a bit of nostalgia in Tanner's voice.

Brad and Tanner had been best friends as kids. They had similar interests, but were polar opposites in appearance. Where Brad was of medium height, blond, blued-eyed, and somewhat baby-faced, Tanner stood tall, dark and brooding, but sinfully handsome.

She and Tanner had known each other since kindergarten, but didn't hook up until midway through high school. As a young girl, she had adored him from afar. Once she got to know him though, she discovered that he was far from a small-town bad boy. He carried deep respect for his family and friends, and he offered his assistance freely. And yet, when she'd needed him most, when she should have leaned on his broad shoulders, she hadn't allowed herself to let him help her.

"So, what do you do?" Brad's question jostled her out of her memories.

"I manage one of the restaurants at the hill."

"What brings you back home?" Matt's question sent Tanner's gaze traveling around the group until it reached

Molly. Trapped by those damn swirls in his eyes, she held her breath, waiting for his next words. "I'm buying a restaurant."

"Cool. Where's the restaurant? Up at the hill or in Vancouver?"

His eyes darkened. "Actually, it's in Ottawa."

Molly gasped and covered her mouth with one hand, turning it into a cough to cover up her surprise. Exclamations and questions abounded. Molly tried to pay attention to the conversation as Matt grilled Tanner about his plans, but once again, a hive of bees had taken up residence between her ears.

He was moving back, would be living in Ottawa. Oh, Lord. Her body sizzled—with excitement or fear, she didn't know which. Most days she considered it a large city. She could avoid him—right? But it was also small enough that no matter where he lived, she would be a mere twenty to forty minutes away. Being so close to him, and not being with him, would kill her.

For her part, Molly had never gotten over him. How could she? He had been her first love, her first lover. She had believed they'd be together forever. Funny how forever isn't very long.

As the conversation droned on around her, Molly slipped back to one special night. The night she had never forgotten. Not a single word, not a single touch. She remembered each and every second. It was the night she resurrected often, the only thing that could get her through to tomorrow when she became immersed in remembering everything that she'd lost.

CHAPTER THREE

Over Ten Years Ago- A never forgotten moment.

TAKING HER HAND, TANNER LED HER TO A secluded spot at the north end of the beach, a private nook nestled amongst the trees. The rest of their friends were back at the campsite, arguing over who won that last game of cards.

When they reached the perfect spot, he released his hold on her hand to lay out the blanket. With a flick of his wrists, he let it fly out before it settled on the grass. He unzipped the sleeping bag, opened it and laid it flat over the blanket. Kicking off his shoes, he crawled between the blankets of the makeshift bed and reached out to her. She laid her hand in his. With a playful tug, he hauled her down beside him and wrapped the sleeping bag snug around the both of them.

Lying side by side, hands clasped under their heads, they gazed up at the star-studded sky. Water lapped at the shoreline, soothing her, lulling her into a sensuous, romantic state. The chirps of a few crickets and the occasional splash of a frog or fish jumping into the water were the only disruptions in their cozy little universe. The scent of Tanner tickled her nose. He never used cologne, just Irish Spring and him.

She rolled her head to peer at him. He lay there, staring at her.

"This is perfect," she whispered.

Without a word, he rolled to his side and canted over her,

brushing his lips across hers. His were soft, his touch tender. She couldn't resist opening her mouth, allowing his tongue to slide inside and dance with hers.

He raised a hand to cup her face as he deepened the kiss.

She reached up and twined her arms around his neck, pulling until his chest fell onto hers. His heart thudded against her. Wrapped together, she surrendered to him.

After a passionate embrace, he ended the kiss and cradled her in one arm while the other rested against her lower belly. His gaze held hers as he inched his hand under her sweater, his fingers tiptoeing in a feather-light touch to cover her breast.

She arched her body, pushing her breast into his grasp.

He bent down to devour her mouth again, their teeth clacking together. She giggled. When he withdrew, she gasped at the hot searing look in his eyes. The desire to laugh disappeared. In the moonlight, his eyes were darker than the night. His chest rose and fell with each breath.

"Come here." Tugging her to a sitting position, he pulled her sweater over her head and dispensed with her bra. Then he laid her back down. The contrast of his tender caresses to the heated attack of his mouth pushed her own arousal to somewhere between a simmer and a boil. He shimmied down her body, taking the tip of one breast into his mouth. After lavishing it with licks and gentle nips, he switched to the other, sucking it hard.

The cover had slipped off and a cool breeze blew over their bodies, drying their already dampening skin. She hardly noticed. Her shiver had nothing to do with the temperature.

"Oh, yes," she groaned.

He flicked one taut nipple with his tongue while pinching the other between his thumb and finger. When she could take no more, she grabbed his face between her hands and brought his mouth back to hers for a scorching kiss.

Pausing for breath, he stared down at her, his eyes smoldering. His voice had a low, husky quality when he spoke. "I love you, Molly. This time next year, we'll be finished with school, and we can be married. Start our life together, have babies, grow old together."

She could only nod. Her breath caught, held. A moan passed his lips as he dipped back to her breasts. When he moved away, her nipples were hardened, distended, and ultra-sensitive. They glistened in the moonlight.

He unfastened her jeans and slipped a hand down inside her panties, cupping her mound while he continued to feast on her nipples. She trembled when he crooked a finger, running it along her moist slit.

He groaned. "You're wet."

Her cheeks heated at his observation.

His tenderness overwhelmed her as he eased a finger inside, leisurely pumping it in and out. Pleasure zinged along her nerves. When he withdrew, she mewled at the loss until he slid a tiny bit higher to tap her clitoris.

Gasping, a wave of sensation rolled through her body, and she jerked her hips, seeking more. He rubbed her clit, round and round in tiny circles. She tensed her thighs, the tingles of an impending orgasm blossoming. He stopped, kneeling back to peel her jeans off.

As he stood to remove his own clothes, she contemplated

his body. Her breath caught in awe every time. At twenty-two, he was in his prime—big, muscular, and strong. Her fingers itched to trace the contours of his hard stomach.

Her gaze travelled lower.

He threw his clothing aside and put a condom over his straining erection. His hands shook.

You'd think this was their first time.

Straddling her hips, he sank to his knees. Lowering to settle his body over hers, he supported his weight on his forearms. At the moment of impact, skin to skin, a tremor rolled through her. The hair on his legs tickled. He pressed the warmth of his chest against her breasts. The hard length of his cock rested hot and heavy against her sex.

She quivered. In his arms, she was complete.

His eyes glowed with passion. He placed soft kisses on the side of her neck, her collarbone, and the tip of each breast, sliding his body lower, making his way down her stomach to her belly button. He dipped his tongue in and swirled it around.

A sensual shiver danced over her skin.

Grasping her hips in both hands, he continued his journey. He shifted until his shoulders were wedged tight between her thighs. Then he stopped. Hot little puffs of air tickled her exposed flesh.

She glanced down her body. Tanner lay there, staring at her intimate parts. She remembered the embarrassment she'd felt the first time he'd gone down on her. It hadn't taken long before it turned to exquisite torture and then mind-numbing bliss, something she anticipated each time they made love.

She heard him exhale as he placed the lightest of kisses on her clit, a butterfly touch at first, barely there. Tease. He applied the smallest amount of pressure, and she groaned. He swiped his tongue down through her slit, and back up, capturing the cream that flowed free.

"God, you taste good."

She couldn't resist. "You work in the restaurant business, and the only word you can come up with to describe taste is *good*? Not very impressive."

"I'm a waiter. But you wait. One day I'll own my own place."

"Yes, I believe you will, Tanner Daivies. So you better find more flattering ways to describe the things you like."

He laughed and laid a hand on each of her thighs, pushing them apart, settling into a more comfortable position between them. "How about divine, heavenly, or, my personal favorite, fucking fabulous." Placing his mouth over her sex, he began to lap in earnest. A growl of contentment rumbled through his chest, vibrating through her body, adding to her pleasure.

She clenched her fists in the blanket on either side of her. Her hips rose of their own accord to meet his mouth. Gasping for air, her body quaked with excitement.

He returned to her clit, first pressing his tongue flat against it, and then pulling it into his mouth, as he applied gentle suction.

She stiffened. A delicious quiver skimmed across her skin. Stars exploded behind her eyelids as her orgasm rolled over her fast and hard. When the fireworks ended, she pried them open to see him poised over her.

"Are you okay?"

She nodded. Better than. "I can't decide if I want to return the favor or move straight to the main act." Her words came out a throaty croak. "But, I think I'd prefer to have you inside me, tonight, right now."

A groan rumbled through his chest, and he dropped down over her, until the head of his cock butted against her slick opening. Tanner pushed into her, one slow inch at a time, his arms shaking.

Anxious, Molly closed her eyes and grasped his forearms. She tilted and lifted her lower half, forcing him to plunge deep, and gasped at the fullness, at the ecstasy of feeling stretched around his hard, thick cock.

"Molly."

Releasing her breath, she opened her eyes.

He peered down at her, his eyes wide, his mouth hanging open.

"What?" Under normal circumstances, she didn't play an aggressive role, but tonight, for some reason, she didn't want slow and easy. "Please, don't stop now. I really need you."

He blinked. Then he started to move and soon found a rhythm that left her panting and desperate. Each deep thrust sent shards of arousal spinning through her body. She explored his face, fascinated by the grimace of sublime male lust reflected there. His eyes closed, his skin flushed, and his lips turned in on each other.

As his hips started pumping faster, his face changed, became harder, his skin tightening across his cheeks. Sweat beaded on his forehead, and he bared his teeth.

She moaned, surprised when another climax began spiraling from within.

Tanner grunted and pushed deep. His cock pulsed inside her.

She gripped his arms and cried out when the power of his release pushed her over the top to ride the wave with him. A sensation of warmth flowed through her, spilled from her.

Clouds had passed in front of the moon, blocking the light. Tanner collapsed on top of her, breathing heavy. After catching his breath, he stood and stepped a few feet away to dispose of the condom. He returned to their bed and drew the sleeping bag snug over them. Molly lay cuddled against his side. Secure in his arms, she fell asleep under the stars.

* * *

Present Day

"Molly?"

She jumped. "Excuse me?"

"I said, what about you?" Tanner raised his voice above the others around the table. She had drifted off, a dreamy expression on her face. From the other end of the table, she lifted her head and turned, her gaze swinging to catch his. Her eyes were wide, and he caught a glimpse of unguarded yearning on her face before she managed to mask it.

Her face flushed a deep red. What had put that color in her cheeks? What was going on inside that pretty head? "What have you being doing with your life?" And more important, he needed to know what her plans were after this weekend.

While Tanner had been fielding questions about his time out west and his plans for the restaurant, his small circle of friends brought him up to date on the happenings within their own lives as well as those of other people he'd grown up with. As they spoke, more guilt piled on top of what already sat like a stone in his belly as he realized how much he'd missed. Friends married and having kids, some getting divorced, others gone from this earth. Maybe fate had intervened, bringing him back before it was too late.

His joy over her initial reaction to his news lost its brightness when her air of excitement turned to something that resembled fear and then worry. After that, she seemed to lose interest in the conversation around her. Other than that brief greeting, they'd had no time to speak in private. He needed to get her alone. And, then he intended to find out, once and for all, what changed ten years ago. Why the sudden desire to spread her wings without him at her side. And why she appeared so panicked now.

"Oh, me?" Her voice squeaked, and she cleared her throat. "I…um…stayed in Ottawa after graduation. Initially I worked for the paper, you remember that one I interned with? Now I write and edit for a national magazine."

"What about your family?"

For a moment, the light died in her eyes. She gave herself a little shake and focused on him again. When she did, shadows replaced the dreamlike trance.

He became aware of the quiet. So focused on Molly, he'd forgotten they weren't alone. Now he realized how loud silence could be. He glanced around the table to confirm that everyone had stopped talking. A few looked toward Molly; the others concentrated on the drink in their hands.

"My brother is married and lives out in Vancouver. They have a daughter, Alyssa—she's two." She shuddered through a deep breath, but gathered her strength. "My parents were killed in a head-on collision about three years ago on their way to the summer camp."

Her quiet statement and the lackluster gaze in her eyes conveyed the lingering pain. With her parents gone, and her brother out west, she had no other family in the area. He hurt for her.

"I'm sorry. I didn't know."

Matt leaned over to nudge her with his shoulder, a gentle show of compassion.

She shrugged. "It's been three years." Her gaze darted to his. Her eyes sparkled with unshed tears.

A few tears slipped over to run unnoticed down her cheeks. She lifted her eyes and caught him staring. She flinched. A mysterious expression flitted across her face before she dropped her head and wiped at her cheeks.

"Okay, folks." Colleen clapped her hands and stood. "It's starting to get dark. Brad, Tanner, you guys gather wood and start a fire while there's still enough light to see, and the rest of us will clean up. Then we'll grab fresh drinks and move over to the fire." A round of nods and murmurs of agreement followed.

Molly jumped up, grabbed some empty plates, and headed for the kitchen tent—the other women not far behind.

Tanner let her scramble away before he pushed away from the table. More was going on than the grief of losing her parents. Something seemed off. He'd expected her to avoid him, maybe treat him like a stranger, but her actions went beyond that. She looked like a frightened doe.

Had there been another guy after all? Did she regret their breakup? Maybe there was hope for him yet. One thing he knew for sure. Until he knew where he stood, all of his plans could wait.

CHAPTER FOUR

HAVING DONNED SWEATERS OR LIGHT COATS TO ward off the evening's chill, Molly and her friends gathered around the fire. She let the comfort of tradition and life-long friendships engulf her. The sounds of crackling campfires interspersed with bursts of voices and laughter, drifting to them from the darkness. Within the boundaries of their own site, music played loud enough to hear, but low enough so as not to disrupt their neighbors. The smell of roasting marsh-mallows wafted through the air from another site. A startled yelp followed by a round of giggles made Molly smile. Oh, to be young again—the thrill of telling secrets and ghost stories in the dark confines of a tent.

Brad stoked the flames while arguing with Matt over the quality of movies they'd seen in recent weeks, and Violet passed around drinks. Molly stayed on the sidelines, sipping her vodka cooler, staring into the flames, trying to ignore Tanner. He strolled over and sat beside her, but didn't say a word.

She ached to shift closer, to bask in the warmth emanating from his body. It would be so easy to lean against him and absorb the comfort and strength she knew she'd find in his embrace. So simple to fall into patterns of the past, as though ten years hadn't slipped by.

But she no longer had that right. What if there were a girl-friend or a Mrs. Tanner Daivies out there, waiting for him? The notion made her cringe.

Jealousy? She almost laughed. She had no right to be jealous. She'd made her decisions. She'd pushed Tanner away because at the time she'd thought it the best option. One of them deserved to achieve their dreams.

She'd had a few boyfriends over the years. Nothing serious though. Work became her excuse to keep men at a distance.

"Do you still enjoy living in Ottawa, Molly?" His voice surprised her out of her musings.

She licked her lips. "Yes, I do. It's a pretty city and close to home. Or at least, what I consider home."

"Do you still live in the same apartment?"

"No."

He picked at the label on his beer bottle. "Do you get a chance to visit your brother often?"

She sighed. "Not as often as I'd like. We talk on the phone every other week. I went out to visit when Alyssa was born." She paused for a moment, her heart skipping a beat. She had been within miles of Tanner. She gave herself a mental shake. "Todd had a hard time after Mom and Dad's accident. He couldn't stick around here—said there were too many memories." She shrugged. "I couldn't seem to leave."

"My parents never said anything."

"I'm sure they figured you wouldn't care." She swiveled her head to meet his eyes for the first time since he sat down.

* * *

A reflection of the flames shimmered in her eyes.

"Molly." Glancing at his friends around the campfire, Tanner lowered his voice. "We need to talk." He didn't know what, if anything, the others knew about their breakup, but this conversation should be in private. "Let's go for a walk." He stood and held out his hand.

She hesitated.

"Please."

After a painfully long moment, she placed her small hand within his. He helped her to her feet and, keeping a firm hold on her, tugged, urging her to follow as he led her out to the road and away from their campsite.

Once they were a safe distance from the others, he released her, sticking his fingers inside the pockets of his hoodie.

She inched to the edge of the roadway to put distance between them.

"It's been a long time, Molly. I want you to know that I'm over it. I'm over what happened. How it ended. But I do need to understand. I need to know. Why did you break up with me? I thought we had a good thing." He focused on her face. Without the aid of the campfire, he tried to search her eyes in the darkness, hoping he might somehow read her mind. "I never forgot you." Not for a day in the ten years since he'd seen her, had he forgotten how she looked, what she smelled like. How good it felt to hold her, to touch her.

To kiss her.

To make love to her.

Raw, undiluted pain filled her eyes. It was a brief flash, and his gut clenched at the token glimpse.

"I don't know what to say to you."

He stepped in front of her and stopped, swiveling around to face her. She stumbled a bit on the gravel to avoid crashing into him. His hands clenched into fists in his pockets—the need to take her in his arms overwhelming. "Look at me."

She lifted her chin, her head slowly tilting back until the features of her face were revealed. Even in the darkness, he saw uncertainty and panic struggling to stay buried behind those wide eyes. Regret sucker-punched him, but he couldn't let it go that easily. After ten long years, he deserved answers.

Tanner grabbed her hand again, spun on his heel, and dragged her toward a path leading into the trees. She balked, pulling backward. He stopped again. "We should talk somewhere we won't be interrupted." Unrelenting, he leveled her with a look.

She lifted her shoulders and let them fall in a slow, fake shrug of indifference.

It had been a long time since he'd been into the park, but he remembered this footpath well. It wound around and would eventually come out behind where they were camped. She followed him until they came to a secluded spot a few feet off the main path. He walked over to a large tree, propped his back against it, shoved his hands in his pockets again, and braced one foot against the tree, hoping to appear casual.

Taking slow, cautious steps, she crept closer, stopping when she stood a few feet before him. "So you're moving to Ottawa."

"Actually, the deal's not done yet."

"But you said—"

"I know what I said, Molly. I do want to move back. But it depends on you."

"On me? What does it have to do with me?"

"Are you seeing anybody?" The iridescent glow from the

full moon filtered down through the branches, providing enough light for him to see her, but with her head ducked, her features were in shadow. He couldn't see enough of her face or her eyes. He was desperate to see her eyes.

"Not that it's any of your business. But no. Not at the moment."

"I'm not either."

She cast him a quick look of surprise. "Why aren't you? You're handsome and, from what I gather, successful. Why aren't you married or committed to some lucky girl?"

He reached out and grabbed her hand, yanking her closer to him.

Gasping, she fell into his chest.

He gathered her close, spinning around to place her against the tree while he leaned in close to ensure she stayed put. She stiffened, surprise in her eyes.

"I've never forgotten you or what we had. You meant everything to me." He put it out there. The pain he'd held in since that day she'd told him it was over, laced his words.

Molly dropped her gaze. "I never meant to hurt you."

Shifting to the left, she made a move to step away from the tree, away from him, but he edged in close, stalling her. He placed his finger under her chin, tipping her face toward the moonlight. He gazed down into her eyes. "Why then? Why did you end it the way you did?"

"I had to... I... Never mind, I just had to." She trembled as she choked out the last.

"I don't understand. Did I do something wrong? Did I hurt you somehow?" His mind raced over their past, as it had many times, trying to figure out what happened. When things changed.

"Of course not." Her conviction put him at ease, a little bit at least.

"Did somebody else do or say something?" Unexpected rage ripped through him. Good God, had somebody hurt her?

"No. No, it wasn't anything you or anybody else did." She tried to pull out of his grasp.

He held steadfast, closing the distance until his chest grazed hers. He pinned her to the tree.

"Please. Let me go."

"I want answers."

"I can't—"

Standing this close to her, for the first time in years, her heart beating a rapid flutter against his chest did wild things to his body. His heartbeat sped up, sweat popped out on his forehead, and his cock hardened to steel. He dropped his gaze to her mouth. Her lush lips parted, warm breaths blew out in little spurts, fluttering against his neckline. He knew he shouldn't rush this. He'd come with a plan to get her back, if she'd take him. But no way could he stop.

"I want the truth. I suppose I can wait a little longer if you're not ready." For answers. He could wait for answers. Touching her, tasting her, was a different thing altogether. "But I do have something I need to give you." He hesitated, questioning his intention. Screw it. "I'm sorry, but I can't resist, and you're too desirable."

He bent his head low, paused, and pressed his lips to hers. It should have been gentle, but it wasn't. Unless she pushed him away, or told him no, the need to kiss her was vital, her taste essential.

She stilled.

He tensed, expecting her to do just that when she raised her arms and placed her palms against his chest. He held his breath, his body trembling while he waited. A heavy sigh escaped her mouth, and she curled the tips of her fingers into his shirt. With a soft whimper, she lured him closer, leaning into his body, taking his kiss.

A flood of emotions strangled him—anger, relief, basic sexual need. Pressing his highly aroused body solidly against hers, he flattened his palms against the tree on either side of her head. A moan rose from his chest. He swept his tongue inside her mouth, dueling with hers. He touched the soft insides of her cheeks and the smooth surface of her teeth, absorbing her unique essence, which was even better than he remembered. He drew back to lick along her bottom lip, placing small kisses at the corners, and then dove back in for more, angling for a closer connection. A sense of urgency began to build.

God, he'd missed this.

His erection strained against his jeans, the extent of his arousal staggering him. He let his hands drop to rest on the slight swell of her hips. Sheltered in this dark spot, with only the nocturnal animals scampering in the brush and the distant sound of campers to keep them company, he willed his body to relax and enjoy the absolute delight of having this woman in his arms once again. He smoothed his hands up her sides, coming around to hold the weight of her breasts.

As though they had all night, he touched her, refreshing

41

his memory of how perfect a fit her body was to his. Using the edge of his fingers, he rubbed across her nipples, smiling against her mouth when they responded, turning into rigid points, noticeable even through her layers of clothing. He pinched the tips, swallowing her gasp of pleasure, when she squirmed against him.

Widening his stance and bending his knees, he canted his hips to grind his pelvis against hers. She pushed back, and he hardened even more. God, how much stiffer could he get? Reaching under her shirt, he ran his hands up the softness of her belly to the rim of her bra, pushing it up and over her breasts. They spilled into his hands, free for his exploration.

Excitement coursed through him at the opportunity to touch her velvet skin. He passed the coarse pads of his thumbs across the tips again, grazing her nipples that were now peaked into hard little cherries. Hidden from view, he referred to his memory. He pictured the tops of her breasts in his mind, her satiny skin flushed with arousal, the pale pink nipples turned dark and rosy, ready for the touch of his mouth. He was eager to see them glistening from his kisses.

She moaned, leaning heavy against him.

He slid his hands down her torso, to the top of her jeans, undid the snap, and pushed them down to her knees. He rested one hand against her hip, his fingers spread wide, while he reached between her legs with the other. He found her ready, hot, and creamy.

She parted her legs as far as the pants allowed.

He growled, slipped a finger inside, pushed his palm against her clit, and applied firm pressure.

She mewled and with tentative moves started rubbing herself against his hand.

He slipped another finger in beside the first and starting pumping them in and out.

She bucked, grinding against his hand.

He increased the pace. Faster and faster, he thrust his hand, using his thumb to stimulate her clit.

Her breath came in hard frantic bursts; his lungs worked double-time. It didn't take long. A few firm flicks over her clit, and Molly's back arched, pushing her pussy snug against him, driving his fingers deep. She sucked in her breath as her body convulsed around him.

He held her close while he continued to caress her, using a more gentle touch, remembering how sensitive she would be. He tipped his head back to watch her. He wanted to see her eyes fill with passion, her skin glow with arousal.

Her lashes rested against her cheeks, as her chest rose with each labored breath. Minutes passed until she opened her eyes. They were glazed and unfocused as she glanced around.

In too short a time, clarity returned. He watched it happen. She peered up, her eyes round and wide, shock registering on her face. Then she pushed him away.

Stumbling, she yanked her jeans up, jerked her bra down and her sweater back into place. Not the reaction he was hoping for.

She refused to look at him.

Tanner stepped back, his rock-hard cock begging for relief. His breaths came in heavy pants. His blood boiled beneath his skin. His desire to bury himself deep inside her, to feel her pussy clutching him, left him shaking. He clenched his fists against his thighs. Fuck, he felt like a kid again, trying to grab a quickie before taking his girlfriend home.

"I'm sorry." Well, not really, but now was not the time to tell her that.

"I...we should head back to camp." With trembling hands, she tugged on her sweater, making unnecessary adjustments. Finally, she chanced a quick peek in his direction. Even in the dark, with filtered moonlight shining down on her face, her embarrassment screamed at him. She turned and ran before he could stop her.

In that short glimpse, in addition to the embarrassment, he saw the lingering arousal he *had* been hoping for. He also saw desperation. The embarrassment he understood—what had happened had been unplanned—and the urgent, unexpected depth of their arousal had shaken her. It sure as hell surprised him. However, the despair confused and alarmed him.

He hurried after her. "Wait. Hold up. You shouldn't run down the path in the dark."

Thankfully, she slowed to a walk, although she kept her distance, not saying a word during the short trip back to camp. When they got there, she grabbed an empty seat between Colleen and Violet, leaving him to sit opposite her, near Brad and Matt. Without a glance in his direction, she joined in their banter, feigning interest, obvious in her attempt to appear uninterested to him.

Six months ago, after his last girlfriend left claiming he had commitment issues; he'd examined the state of his life. That's when he discovered he'd never gotten over Molly Simpson.

He'd spent the next few weeks reliving their last few months, trying to figure out where things had gone wrong. He was surprised to realize she had been withdrawn for weeks before he left. Thinking back on it, she'd been less talkative since that last winter break. At the time, he'd chalked it up to finals and her new job at the newspaper. But, something had been wrong. He didn't know it then, but he did now.

Based on her response back by the tree, something still existed between them, a passion he intended to explore. Part of the exploration would be discovering what in the hell happened to his girlfriend ten years ago. The other part considered her plans for her future, or more to the point, *their* future.

CHAPTER FIVE

MOLLY YAWNED. THE MOON OWNED A PLACE HIGH in the sky, lighting up the ground below. Her behavior tonight shamed her. How could she give in so totally, so fast? Make it so easy for him? God, she hadn't seen the man in ten years. And in one night, he had her pressed up against a tree and coming on his hand. What must he think of her? She needed to escape and go over the events of the day, figure out where her resolve had slipped. She hoped Violet wouldn't be in the mood to chat tonight.

"I'm heading to bed." She stifled another yawn. "See you in the morning." Colleen and the others acknowledged her departure with a mixture of waves and mumbled wishes for sweet dreams.

"I think I'll turn in too." Violet rose to join Molly.

They turned toward the tent they were sharing. Keeping her head down, Molly fiddled with her zipper to avoid looking in Tanner's direction.

The girls made a quick trip to the restroom and then settled in for the night. It was cool enough to warrant warm pajamas and socks.

They snuggled into down-filled sleeping bags before Violet's hushed voice broke the silence. "Do want to talk about it?"

"About what?"

"About whatever's bothering you." Violet lay in silence

beside her for a few beats and then shifted and rolled to her side, facing Molly in the dark. "You were there for me all those years ago when my mom and I first moved to town and I had nobody. You're my friend. I want to help."

Molly swallowed. She had the best friends. If only she could tell them. "I'm fine. It was just a shock to see Tanner today."

"Have you spoken to him since he left?"

"Today was the first time in ten years." A very long, perhaps short, ten years.

"I'm here if you need me."

"I know you are. Thank you. You're a good friend."

Violet rolled to her other side. Soon, soft snores drifted across from her side of the tent.

Molly wrestled with her emotions in silence, taking a few deep breaths, trying to calm the trembling. She lay staring at the roof, watching images of tree branches and leaves sway back and forth across the canvas, the shapes distorted by the flickering light of the campfire. Muted conversations and sporadic laughter filtered through the night.

She lifted her hand to her lips, recalling how his lips felt against hers—demanding, yet familiar. She stroked down to her breast, then her stomach, remembering how his hands played her body—gentle, yet familiar. She cupped herself between her legs, calling to mind how it felt to come apart in his arms—explosive, oh, so familiar.

Heat flamed her cheeks. He still had the power to light her body on fire. He remembered where to touch her, how to please her. She had never planned to test the theory, but she had always assumed being in his arms again would resurrect fond memories of her love for the young man he had been.

Instead, his caress invoked the desires of a woman. A woman who had gone too long without the attention of a man. He delivered powerful kisses, as though he had been holding on to them for the last ten years. One simple touch of his lips had ignited the inferno she'd assumed dormant. Lust rushed her brain and closed off every rational notion—except one—her longing to be held and loved again and the desire to know what she'd been missing since he left.

Her toes curled at the memory of her orgasm. She'd been helpless to do anything but accept it, even revel in it, which she did. Thank God her senses had returned before she'd done something stupid—like throw herself at him and beg him to fuck her hard and fast against that tree. She shivered.

He scared her. Not him, he'd never hurt her, but the emotion he seemed to summon with no effort. She'd worked hard to put the past behind her. To bury the hopes and dreams she'd once had.

Molly remembered that night on the beach. God, it seemed like ages ago. She waited for the memories to bombard her. One of the best nights of her life, and ultimately, one of the worst. She often suspected that was the night she conceived Tanner's child.

* * *

Molly jerked awake. Startled, she darted glances around the tent, her ears perked, listening for something out of place. In a tent, the silence of the hour amplified all other sounds. She heard a few of her friends shift positions in their sleep, emitting muffled grumbles as they resettled. Ears straining, she waited. She'd been asleep for a while. The snap and pop of dying embers and the occasional shifting of a broken log were the only noises outside the tent.

The soft hiss of a pulled zipper stole through the night. She tensed. Her breathing stilled as she tried to determine the direction it came from. Somebody shuffled quietly through the campsite, footsteps moving away from the tents, and then nothing for a few minutes. She waited until they returned, coming from the direction of the trees. Probably one of the guys.

The crush of grass underfoot got louder as the steps drew near. They paused when they reached her side of the tent. Tanner. Molly held her breath, waiting for him to move on. When he didn't, she considered that perhaps she was mistaken, but then his knees cracked as he bent down.

"Molly?" His call not more than a whisper. "Are you awake?"

She dared not move, not breathe. Her lungs began to burn. When he received no response, he stood, hesitating for a moment before retreating to his own tent.

She released her breath when she heard him draw the zipper closed behind him. She listened to him settling down again. Relieved, she turned on her side and closed her eyes, willing sleep to return.

When sleep claimed her hours later, she didn't have the pleasure of dreaming about shopping for shoes or handbags or even going back to that night on the beach. She returned to the event that changed everything, the day her hopes and dreams shattered like a broken mirror.

CHAPTER SIX

TANNER STEPPED AWAY FROM THE TENT, stretched his arms over his head, and yawned. His joints cracking couldn't drown out the sound of birds singing and squirrels chattering as they argued over territory. The occasional cloud dotting the otherwise blue sky promised a beautiful spring day. The clanging of pots and the aroma of bacon drifted on the warm breeze. Campers were up and starting their day.

He grabbed a shower at the communal restrooms before the rest of the campground woke up. When he returned, he found Molly awake, absorbed in preparing breakfast. He walked up behind her. "Good morning."

She jumped. "Oh, I didn't hear you. Morning." Keeping her eyes downcast, she kept her back to him.

Going on instinct, he reached around and grasped her chin in his hand. With gentle force, he turned her toward him. The skin around her bloodshot eyes appeared puffy, strained, and pale. She'd been crying. Her eyes widened the tiniest bit before her gaze dropped to the ground.

His eyes narrowed. "What's wrong?"

"Nothing. I'm fine. I didn't sleep well, and I...I need a shower to wake up."

More like she needed an opportunity to escape. "I'll take care of breakfast. You go have a shower while it's not too busy yet."

"Thanks. I'd appreciate that." She backed away from him and leaped to grab her stuff, which she'd already assembled on the picnic table. She rushed off, moving as though demons from hell were on her tail.

No demons. Just him.

She tossed a quick glance back over her shoulder and slowed her pace. Judging by the panic etched on her delicate features, she wanted to run. He stood, watchful until she disappeared around the bend. Damn it.

He walked over to stow his gear in the tent. Brad lay on his stomach, his face ground into his pillow, oblivious to Tanner going in and out of the tent. He returned to the kitchen tent to finish breakfast preparations.

Sleep had been elusive, and not because Brad snored like a diesel engine. He hadn't been able to stop thinking about Molly. About kissing her and making her come. She'd responded to him like never before. She had become a beautiful woman, one he wanted to get to know all over again. He was determined to spend more time with her, much more time before the weekend came to a close.

When Molly returned, she maintained her distance. The smell of cooking sausages permeated the air as they sat sipping coffee, waiting for the others to join them. She turned on a radio, tuned to the local station, and hummed along with the songs—an obvious excuse to avoid conversation. He refused to be put off. He would simply bide his time.

The tempting breakfast odors, or the craving for caffeine, soon roused the rest of their party. They rolled out of their tents, some groggy, some chipper, all starving. After gobbling down eggs, sausage, and toast, they sat around the picnic table, drinking an assortment of beverages.

Tanner noticed Sam and Olivia sharing a secret smile. Best friends since the cradle, they started dating in high school, but delayed getting married until they both completed university and secured full-time jobs. Guilt assailed him, one more time, over the fact that he didn't come home for their wedding. He hadn't even called.

Sam cleared his throat, attracting everyone's attention. Looking a little bashful, he turned to them. "Liv and I have news we wanted to share with you guys." He glanced at his wife, an endearing smile on his face. "We're having a baby."

A stunned silence followed for about a millisecond before the other girls squealed and stumbled over themselves to get around the table to hug Olivia, while the men damn near knocked Sam off the bench patting him on the back. Only Molly didn't rush to congratulate the happy couple. In fact, her face lost what little color she had left. That mysterious expression he'd glimpsed the previous night returned, before she rose and left the table. Other than a concerned glance from Colleen, nobody but Tanner noticed her quick, but quiet, exit. He stood to follow her.

With her head down, she sprinted past the other campers, taking the same route from the night before. He hung back, but kept her in his sights. About one hundred yards in, she veered off the path and ducked into the trees.

Tanner found her in a small clearing hidden by a handful of large bushes. She sat on a large boulder, knees up, arms curled around them, hiding her face in an attempt to muffle her sobs. Her whole body trembled. The sheer agony in her posture, in her cries, pierced his heart. He crept closer. When he was within a few feet, he called out, keeping his voice low, his tone soothing. "Molly, sweetheart, what's wrong?"

She scrambled away from the rock and spun to face him. Her eyes were wide. Tears flowed down her face. Her panic turned to grief when she realized it was him. A heartfelt sob wracked her body, and she started to crumble to the ground. He rushed forward, catching her before her knees hit the dirt, and gathered her into his arms.

At first, she resisted, her body coiled like a spring. She pushed at his chest, but he held firm, clutching her tighter through her brief struggle. Defeated, she went limp and fell into his embrace, wrapping her arms around his waist and tucking her head under his chin.

"Hush, honey…it's okay." He pressed his face into her hair as he cuddled her close. Her body shook with the force of her sobs. "It's okay." Keeping his hold on her, he shifted and moved a few steps backward to lean against the boulder.

With her secure in his arms, he rocked back and forth, for what seemed like hours until she stopped crying and her body sagged against his. When she lifted her hand to wipe her face, he let her pull away, certain she'd try to hide from him again. "Do you want to tell me what that was about?"

She peered into his eyes. Blinked.

He waited.

She dropped her gaze to the ground, and then raised her hands, covering her face for a few moments. She started to massage her temples. Two fingers on each hand moving in slow circles at each side of her head.

He continued to wait.

She finally managed a couple of deep breaths and then dropped her hands to her sides.

"There's something I need to tell you. Something I should have told you a long time ago. But I can't carry this secret around anymore. Not if I want to be happy for my friends. Happy for you and what you've achieved."

Shit, what kind of secret could have her so worked up?

She strolled a few feet away. Squaring her shoulders, she spun around to face him. "The reason I broke up with you—"

An array of emotions played across her face. Pain. Fear. Sadness. Pain, again. She closed her eyes. When she opened them and stared straight into his, they were filled with resigned determination.

"I had a miscarriage, Tanner."

His mouth opened, but no words came out. He cleared his throat a few times and swallowed. A tiny gray rabbit scampered out of the brush and froze when it spotted them. Its nose twitched as it tested whether they were friend or foe. Making its choice, it scampered away.

"Excuse me?" he finally said. "What do you mean? When were you pregnant?"

Molly clasped her hands together, wrung them, and started to pace back and forth. She stopped. Her voice shook when she spoke. "I found out I was pregnant before our last Christmas together."

He stumbled two steps and curled at the waist, his breath

expelled in a rush. He fought to suck in some badly needed oxygen. Desperate to make sense of what she had said, he put up his hand. "Wait. That last…you were pregnant?" He paused for a long moment while the thoughts in his head swirled. A baby. "You lost a baby. Our baby. And you didn't tell me?" Ten fucking years ago. A baby. *Their* baby.

"Why didn't you tell me when you found out?"

"I planned to tell you over the holidays. It was supposed to be a surprise. I didn't want to distract you during exams. I was distracted enough for the both of us."

"And what about after exams?" He gritted his teeth.

"By then it was…too late." Her voice trailed off.

"And then?"

"I never found a good time." Her voice had softened to a near whisper.

"Too late? A good time? Fuck, Molly." He caught himself before he yelled. He paused to take a calming breath. "It's never too late to tell a guy he's going to be a father."

"It is when he's not going to be one anymore."

He stalked toward her and grasped her shoulders in his hands. "There's certainly time to tell him when it's gone."

Tanner pushed the words out, leaving a bitter taste on his tongue. His tone sounded unforgiving, even to his own ears, but he didn't give a damn.

She paled and tried to step away, but he held her arms pinned at her sides.

He finally let his hands drop away and retreated a few steps, running his fingers through his hair. "Christ, I thought we loved each other. Would have a future together." His voice cracked. He swallowed around the sudden lump in his throat. "How could you not tell me something so fucking important?" He stomped around the clearing.

She waited him out.

When he regained a modicum of restraint, he circled back to face her. "Is that why you wouldn't see me at Christmas?"

She nodded.

"What happened?" His voice, thunderous in the silence of the small clearing, made her jump. Even the wildlife stilled.

"A few days before Christmas, I woke up bleeding. My parents rushed me to the hospital. I hadn't told them yet either." Her face flamed red, and she bit her lip before she looked away.

His insides ached. When he spoke, his voice came out more severe than he intended, raw with emotion. "Why didn't you tell me? I would have been there for you. Damn it, I *should* have been there for you."

"I was scared, Tanner. I didn't realize what was happening. Then, I didn't want pity, and I couldn't face the possibility of you blaming me either."

"Blame you? Blame you for what? You didn't give me the chance to do anything. I don't know how I would have reacted, but I wouldn't have blamed you for getting pregnant. Christ, I was there too." He drove his fingers through his hair again. "You should have trusted me. I would have helped you through it." He paced the clearing. "How far along were you?"

"Almost four months."

"Four months? Four fucking months, and you didn't say a word to me in all that time?"

"I'd only known for a few weeks."

A painful sense of loss ruptured his soul. Not for a baby he'd known nothing about, but for not having the opportunity to share her grief, to comfort his girlfriend when she needed him most. Parenthood came with obligations. Losing the chance to become a parent also came with responsibilities. She'd taken away his responsibility.

"We'd been living together for over three years. Didn't I mean anything to you? Didn't you love me at all? Didn't you trust that I could help you when you were hurting?" He paused, his body shuddering on his next exhale. "It was my baby too." Spinning on his heel, he walked over to one of the boulders that ringed the area and, with his back to it, slid down to the ground.

* * *

Molly rested against a tree, staying while Tanner wrestled with his emotions, struggling to absorb her confession. Maybe he didn't want her here, but she couldn't leave him just yet. She remained quiet but watchful as tears slipped from the corners of his eyes to run unchecked down his cheeks. He appeared totally unaware, or unconcerned. He'd sit for a bit, jump up and pace the small clearing, and then return to perch on one of the boulders. He repeated the routine, oblivious to or most likely ignoring her presence.

When at last he stood and simply stared at her, she jumped up, brushing pine needles and grass from her backside and legs. For long moments, he continued to observe her, no expression on his face, but his suffering was palpable. She waited.

He strode toward her, his gait stiff. He stopped an inch away from her toes and regarded her in silence, his eyes dark, shuttered.

She trembled, unsure what his next action would be. Would he yell? Grab her by the shoulders and shake her in anger?

He hesitated before reaching out.

She held her breath.

Tanner placed his hands on her shoulders and pulled her into his arms.

This time, she stepped into his embrace willingly.

He didn't utter a word. His gentleness unraveled her. Every ounce of pain, the guilt, the heartbreak, but most of all the relief of finally sharing it with somebody, with the one somebody she should have, exploded out of her in deep, gut-wrenching sobs. The suddenness and extent of her grief surprised her, embarrassed her, but she couldn't stop.

She cried for a tiny life that never had a chance, for a dear friend who lost ten years with his family, and she cried for missing the opportunity of a lifetime to spend the rest of her life with the only man she ever loved.

CHAPTER SEVEN

MOLLY'S SOBS SWITCHED TO SOFT HICCUPS. He cupped her face in his hands and tipped her head back. He wiped away the remaining tears and then lowered his head and joined his lips to hers. He licked along the fold and into the corners of her mouth, sipping at the salty moisture captured there. If only he could absorb her pain.

A shudder racked her body as a sigh escaped. He dipped his tongue inside her mouth, stroking the tip of her tongue. Passion for this beautiful woman surged through him, leaving him shaken with the depth of his emotions for her. Deepening the kiss, heated desire swelled his cock to uncomfortable proportions.

Draping her arms around his neck, Molly pushed her fingers through his hair, made fists, and pulled his head down to hold him in place.

He explored her warmth as though they had all day. His mind raced with a variety of things he wanted to do, but he put the mental brakes on, not wanting to risk her running again.

She pressed her body close. Her nipples beaded into hard little points, drilling his chest. She began to pant, stuttering every so often, the aftereffect of crying for such a long time. Her tongue tangled with his.

His memories guided him as he withdrew from her lips to plant kisses from behind her ear, down to her collarbone.

He licked his way back to a particularly sensitive spot below her ear.

Her head fell back, exposing her throat. She twisted her head to the other side.

He'd happily kiss her wherever she wanted him to. Starting at the hollow of her throat, he swept his tongue along the soft skin on her neck.

A moan bubbled from her lips, and her body quivered in his arms.

He repeated the process on the other side before returning to recapture her mouth in a bruising kiss. He drilled into her mouth and anchored his hips to hers, his plea blatant.

She tilted back and peered up, her eyes open, the lids heavy.

Excitement sped through his body.

"I need you." His request rough, his throat scratchy, sounded more caveman-like than he was comfortable with, but he got the point across.

* * *

Molly scanned the area around them, ensuring their little oasis remained private. Other than rabbits, squirrels, and the occasional bird, they were alone.

The sun filtered through the trees creating a patchwork of shade. Earth and aroused male were the two scents strong enough to interest her. Her hands trembled as she reached out for Tanner's shirt, her fingers fumbling with the snaps. A deep yearning overwhelmed her. Here, now, with nature their single witness she craved him. She hoped once sated, the hunger would go away. Maybe then she'd finally find peace and could move on.

Telling him the truth smashed down a barrier she hadn't realized existed. She still had plenty to explain, to apologize for, but right now, at this small moment in time, this was what she wanted, and to hell with the consequences. She needed him. She had waited long enough.

She ran her hands over his chest, stopping to rub his small brown nipples into hard little pebbles, before she tipped forward to sample a taste of his flesh. She followed each brush of her lips with a flick of her tongue and a gentle bite, elated when he sucked in his breath, hissing through his teeth. Encouraged, she worked her way first across his very fine upper chest and then down the middle toward his taught belly.

His muscles tightened beneath her fingers as she made her way down his body until she kneeled in front of him, small pebbles and pine needles digging into her knees. She peeked up through her lashes. She raised her hands as high as she could reach, and in a slow, sensual glide, raked her nails down his stomach.

He quivered, delighting her with a lusty male groan.

She paused at the waistband of his jeans. Tilting her head back, she stared deep into his eyes and licked her lips.

His breath caught. His intent gaze fixated on her tongue, his pupils dark and dilated.

She imagined she could hear the pounding of his heart.

She undid his snap and reached around to grab the back of the waistband, pushed it over his hips, down to his knees. She sat back on her heels. She'd never seen a sexier, more vibrant man. His erection stretched long, thick, and heavy in its aroused state. The dark plum-colored head spilled precum from the tiny slit. Wrapping one hand around his length, she moved in tight, firm strokes up and down. His skin soft as velvet and warm, he seemed to pulse in her grip. She flexed the fingers on her other hand and raised it to cradle his balls.

Molly leaned closer, her tongue slipping out to lick at the pearl of liquid gathered at the tip. Her eyes drifted closed as she swallowed. She opened wide and covered the head of his cock, filling her mouth until it rested atop the bed of her tongue. Then she closed her lips, surrounding him.

His breath whooshed out of his body as he sagged against the large boulder holding him up. She smiled; her lips stretched wide around him and closed her eyes in ecstasy. Humming her appreciation of his salty taste and male scent, she moved her mouth up and down in slow, deep glides, taking him to the back near her throat on every other stroke.

He thrust his hands in her hair. Using gentle manipulation, he tried to control her speed.

She consumed him, taking him as deep inside as she dared, and then withdrew, applying suction when she neared the top. Again and again, she repeated the maneuver, twisting her head on the occasional upward movement to provide pressure at different points.

He strengthened his hold and began to thrust his hips, his cock tunneling in and out of her mouth. "Oh, man, honey, that feels fantastic. Your mouth is so hot."

Molly eased back to run her tongue around the top, stopping to flick against the sensitive spot under the rim. She caressed his balls in the palm of her hand, massaging them with her fingers while she licked and planted kisses around the head.

"More. Suck me some more. Harder."

She nodded, eager to oblige. Oh, yes, this was exactly what the doctor ordered.

One last time with Tanner.

* * *

Tanner leisurely pumped in and out, captivated by the glide of his dick through the circle of her lips. She covered his cock like a heated blanket. He loved to see her mouth around him, his shaft shiny and wet each time she eased back and then swallowed him up again. His balls pulled uptight, the need to come building to an urgent state, but he didn't want to explode in her mouth. It had been too long. He wanted to experience that particular pleasure buried deep inside her body.

With a mixture of regret and anticipation, he gave her hair a firm tug.

She stopped and peered at him with glazed eyes.

The unfocused stare, her face clouded with lust, his cock shoved halfway to the back of her throat, made him growl low and harsh. "I need you to stop. If you keep going, I'll lose it, and I want to come inside you."

He drew back until he fell from her mouth with a soft *pop*. When she pouted and licked her lips, he almost changed his mind. However, his need to taste her won out. The warmth flowing over his fingers last night had been exquisite. Now he wanted her flavor on his tongue. His mouth watered just thinking about it. He wondered if she was as sweet as he remembered.

Yanking up his jeans, but leaving them undone, he reached down to help her stand. He removed her shorts and panties, placing the shorts on the rock to cushion her rear as best he could. He eased her down and knelt before her. Then it was his turn to gaze up.

Face flushed, eyes bright, this gorgeous woman sat perched before him, her lips red and swollen from sucking his cock.

"My turn." He spread her thighs, lifting her legs to place her feet over his shoulders. He inhaled as he surveyed her, intimately spread open before him. Her pussy glistened with dew like droplets. The scent of her arousal fanned the fire in his gut. He bent forward, his tongue flicking out to steal a sample. A moan rose from deep inside as he kissed her silky flesh.

He toyed with her clit, licked along the length of her opening, sucked and nibbled on her engorged lips.

Her body vibrated. With each pass over the aroused little pleasure point, and every dip into her warm entrance, she bucked against his chin.

"Please." She panted. "Make me come."

He chuckled. "Soon."

"Now, Tanner. I need to come now."

He flicked her clit again, enjoying the shivers that travelled through her body, the increased trembling in her legs. He pressed a finger deep inside, her juices seeping out around it. He shoved in a second finger, pumping both in and out while he alternated between licking and sucking on her pussy lips. The walls of her vagina clenched, trying to pull him in deeper. He worked his tongue and fingers faster.

The quake in her thighs increased until at last, her body

clamped down like a vise, clutching his fingers, and she uttered a carnal cry of release.

She spilled onto his tongue, her intoxicating cream covering it. He lapped up every drop he could catch, slowing his strokes to soft sweeps. He remained mindful of her tender skin, but strove to extend the pleasure for as long as possible. Her breathing returned to normal, and a purr of satisfaction reached his ears.

* * *

Molly sagged, her body limp and relaxed, but they weren't finished yet.

He stood, and with his gaze locked on hers, put the fingers he'd had in her pussy, into his mouth. He closed his lips around them and sucked, licking them clean—even the web between each digit.

Her stomach clenched. Oh man, that was hot.

"I need you inside me." There had been no one since Tanner who could make her feel the way he did. Mistake, or not, she couldn't stop herself from wanting it or from taking what he offered.

His eyes darkened as he plucked his wallet from his back pocket and extracted a condom. Pushing his jeans down with one hand, he held the package to his mouth with the other, and ripped it open. His gaze never strayed from hers as he rolled it over his erection.

Jerking her to her feet, he removed her tank top, and spun her around to face the rock. With a firm hand on her back, he urged her to lean forward until her upper body stretched over the surface and she grasped the opposite edge with her fingertips. He stepped in behind and cradled her hips in his hands. With her ass snug against his pelvis, he bent over her back and brushed his lips along the back of her neck, then trailed his tongue down her spine.

She shuddered.

He reached around between her chest and the boulder to rub his palms across her peaked nipples. He pinched them, bringing a sting of pleasure to the tips and a gasp of desire to her lips. Then he removed his hands and, placing one palm against the center of her back, pressed her down to bring the tips of her nipples in contact with rock.

Cool and rough against the hot, hard surface of her nipples was one of the most sensuous things she had ever experienced. Moisture flooded her pussy, and she curled her body, rubbing her chest back and forth. The abrasion alone brought her closer to climax.

From behind, he entered her, inch by thick, hard inch. Her eyes widened, and she grunted low in her throat as he stretched her wide. He pushed until his cock filled her, until his balls tickled her ass.

"God, you're tight." His voice sounded strained; he had to work to get the words out. "You feel so fucking wonderful. I've missed this, sweetheart. I've missed you."

As he withdrew, pulling across sensitive tissue, she whimpered at the emptiness.

Going from simmer to a fast boil, pressure began to build, low in her belly. He plunged back into her depths, withdrew, plunged again. Before he had acted as though they had all the time in the world—now he wasted none.

He quickened his pace, pumping harder, faster, the force of the movement rocking her torso back and forth against the rock. Each drag of her nipples across the boulder heightened the erotic sensations, catapulting her toward orgasm.

She gasped as he drilled into her, his grip no doubt leaving marks on her hips with the force of each thrust. The added stimulation pushed her closer to the edge, sending her to the very precipice, urging her to tumble over.

When he reached around her hips and pinched her clit between his thumb and forefinger, she exploded, shoving her head into the crook of her arm to stifle a scream. Fireworks erupted behind her closed eyelids. She succumbed to the release, blind to her surroundings.

Unrelenting, he continued to fuck her, pounding in hard thrusts until he rammed into her one final time, staying deep, his body shuddering over hers. His hips tight against her behind, he curved protectively over her back, wrapped his arms around her, and pinned his cheek against her spine. His cock stiffened and jerked deep inside her.

* * *

Holy fuck. He had never had an orgasm leave him feeling sucked dry.

Tucked beneath him, Molly dragged in gulps of air. He should get up before he crushed her, but couldn't find the energy to move his limbs. What had happened? What had started out being a revelation about the past, one that had left him hurt and angry, had ended with the best sex of his life.

He needed time to figure everything out, to decide where to go from here. With no small effort, he managed to lift up and back away, needing a little space to pull up his pants and get it together.

A squirrel darted up a nearby tree, chattering his anger at the invasion. Crap. He glanced around. He wouldn't have heard a marching band pass by. He had been so into her that he'd blocked everything else out; including what had brought them here in the first place.

He waited while she pulled her clothes back on. She looked stunned too.

"I didn't hurt you, did I?"

"I'm fine." Her skin glowed a pretty pink, but she didn't avoid his gaze.

He sent up a prayer of thanks. He didn't want her to regret anything. He certainly didn't. How could he? He loved her.

Everything inside him stilled as the realization settled like a quilt around him.

His plans to return to Ontario hinged on her, on whether she would accept him living in the same city, perhaps even work on rebuilding their friendship. He had hoped she might still feel something for him. Guess that question had been answered.

But he hadn't planned to fall in love with her again. Not so soon anyway. Hell, was it even possible? Fuck. Maybe he never stopped.

But what now? She'd kept a major secret from him—her pregnancy. His baby.

He wasn't sure about anything. They had a lot to discuss. He had no idea what she'd been doing, who she'd been seeing in the past years, or what her plans were for the future. But he intended to find out. They had things to work out. And her answers impacted his future.

"We should return to camp." She had redressed. "The others are going to wonder where we went."

Was that regret he heard now? "We need to finish our discussion."

"I know. We will. For now, though—" She waved a hand between the two of them. "This…what happened here is a little overwhelming. I need time before we talk about the rest. Do you mind?"

He did. However, he understood overwhelmed. "Yeah, that's fine. Maybe we can take a walk down to the beach tonight. Talk there?"

A funny look crossed her face. "We'll see."

He reached for her hand. "Fair enough. Come on. Let's go congratulate our friends on their happy news."

He led her through the trees and back to the path. As they neared their campsite, music and laughter reached their ears, and the smell of burgers cooking over an open fire wafted to their noses. His stomach growled. They'd been gone for some time.

She dropped his hand just before their friends spotted them.

The immediate disappointment stung, but it dissipated fast, replaced with hope. He shoved his hands into the pockets of his jeans to discourage or least hide the erection that was building again. He smiled. They would have to work on rebuilding their friendship. He expected it would take time. Time well invested if things worked out the way he hoped.

CHAPTER EIGHT

COLLEEN GLANCED UP IN TIME TO CATCH THEIR arrival. She rose from her chair and walked over, meeting them halfway. "Hey, guys. Where've you been? We missed you after breakfast." Her intent gaze swung back and forth between the two of them. Tanner offered a polite smile, but disclosed nothing. He kept moving. Colleen turned a curious glance back to Molly. "Is everything okay?"

"Yeah." Molly's heart and soul felt much lighter. They weren't healed, but they weren't so broken anymore either.

"Sweetie, you've been crying. Did he say or do something to hurt you?"

"No, nothing like that. Honest." She swallowed and glanced over Colleen's shoulder. Tanner had joined the others and was talking with Sam. "We had some things to work out, and it...got a little emotional. I'm fine." In truth, she felt more than fine. She'd just experienced the best sex of her life—with the hardest orgasm ever—at the hands of the true love of her life.

If only she could have Tanner *in* her life.

"You're sure?"

Molly gave her a reassuring hug. "Yes, I'm sure. Now, let's go get some food. I'm starving."

Before filling her stomach, Molly congratulated her friends. Satisfied she'd expressed true happiness for them without tugging too hard at her own heartstrings; she helped herself to some lunch and grabbed a chair to sit down, ready to sit back and enjoy an afternoon with her friends.

They spent the day playing lawn darts and cards, the girls ganging up against the guys. The men strutting, thumping their chests when they beat the women at darts, claiming the ladies cheated when they won at cards. They listened to favorite bands of the past on somebody's car radio, every now and then stopping to sing a particular chorus aloud together. They laughed at the pleasant memories and cried at a few sad ones. They retold stories of mischief and narrow escapes. They talked about past camping trips. Too bad time didn't come with a rewind button.

The more time she spent with Tanner, the more she ached for him. Old feelings floated to the surface, struggling for purchase. She fantasized of a future with him; however, that's all it could be—a dream. Molly would tell him what happened, all of it, and when the weekend ended, they would go their separate ways.

She'd spent two years working at it, at getting over him, and everything else. With the help of a therapist, she'd dealt with the miscarriage, the death of her parents, and her brother moving away. She'd finally realized she'd done nothing to cause any of it, nor was there anything she could have done to prevent any of it.

With the truth out, it was time to move on now. Her feelings over the pregnancy and its potential long-term effects had inhibited her from pursuing long-term relationships. The shame and guilt of keeping something so important from the one person who could have helped her, the one person who would have shared her grief, left her questioning her ability to commit to anybody.

Molly prayed he would forgive her for not telling him the truth about the pregnancy and the miscarriage. He had a right to be hurt and angry. She understood that. But he had no idea what she'd gone through. The shock of discovery, the terror that he might leave her, the changes to her body, the excitement, the joy, and then terror again. Pain. Physical and mental anguish.

She hoped after this, maybe they'd be friends. She couldn't live in the same city and not be friends.

Friends? Who was she kidding?

* * *

Night folded down around the campground, tucking them into a protective, cozy haven, their tents nothing but dim shadows beyond the rim of light provided by the fire. The background music turned to softer, slower selections, and her friends began to pair off. She envied Sam and Olivia as they stepped beyond the ring of light and turned toward one another, their faces golden in the fire's glow. They cuddled close, swaying to the music, murmuring soft words to each other.

Tanner appeared at her side and bent down. His breath whispered against the shell of her ear. "Dance with me?"

She hesitated, but nodded and rose to her feet.

Taking her hand, he led her a few feet away from the others before pulling her into the shelter of his arms. She laid her head against his chest, closed her eyes and inhaled, storing his scent in her memory bank for later.

He tucked her close. It may have been the drinks she'd consumed, the trip down memory lane, the music...or maybe it was the man. Whatever. She didn't want it to end, not tonight, anyway. In two short days, she'd go back to the city. Alone. Why not take advantage of this small reprieve? She allowed a deep sigh to travel through her body as she rested against him.

Not a word passed between them for a few songs.

Molly found herself daydreaming about unrealistic possibilities when Tanner's husky voice interrupted her. "Let's take a walk."

Her mouth formed a no, but the word never slipped past her lips. If they went off to some secluded spot, there was a high probability they would end up making love again. Mistaking her trembling for being cold, Tanner snuggled her closer and rubbed his hand down her back.

She melted at the warmth flooding her. "I'll just grab a jacket first."

When she turned toward the tent, she realized only Violet, Matt, and Brad remained around the fire, involved in a discussion on the upcoming municipal elections. The others, she presumed, had gone in search of their own private moments.

Molly fetched her coat and returned to Tanner's side. He had his own coat, and he'd thought to bring a blanket and a flashlight. Tucking the blanket under one arm, he reached for her hand with the other.

She followed him through the trees to a path leading to the beach. They made the twenty-minute trek in silence, the flashlight bobbing along in front of them, illuminating the trail ahead. The occasional bout of laughter or music from other sites trickled through the trees. They heard the scampering of four-legged animals anxious to get out of their way. An owl hooted from somewhere high above.

The smell of the lake reached her nose before they broke out of the trees onto the sand and crossed to a formation of rocks that crowded the far northeast corner. Tanner made his way around to the other side where a point beyond a small grouping of trees lay bathed in moonlight. At night, it was breathtaking—and private. He swept out the blanket, laying it on the sand and sat in the center. Memories flooded her. She stood looking down at him for a moment, remembering that long ago night.

She swallowed, toed off her shoes, and sat down beside him.

For a few moments, silence filled the space between them; only the sound of the water hitting the shoreline broke it. Her mind skipped back to this same beach, this same spot, many years ago. A lifetime ago. "It's still beautiful here."

"I want the whole story, Molly." His voice, pitched low, shattered the stillness. "We always practiced safe sex. I never screwed up. I'm certain of that." Based on his rigid position, he was trying hard to contain the anger that tinged his words.

She focused her attention on the sand sifting through her fingers. "I know you were careful. It wasn't anything you did. One of the condoms must have been defective or broke and we didn't realize it. I don't know how it happened, but it did. Don't worry, I don't blame you." She never blamed him.

She paused to take a fortifying breath before she went on.

77

"A few weeks before our exams, I realized I had missed my last period. When I checked the calendar, I realized I'd actually missed a few. So I took a home pregnancy test." She'd never been regular, so she honestly didn't think to pay that close attention. She shrugged. "I didn't want to say anything until I had a chance to confirm it, and I didn't want to alarm you in case it was a false positive." She chanced a quick peek in his direction. He sat, facing forward, looking out over the water. He appeared indifferent, but his stiff bearing said otherwise—his full attention remained riveted on her. She returned hers to the sand.

"We were studying for exams and making plans for Christmas. I was heading home before you, so I figured I'd get it confirmed and then surprise you." However, by then she'd known in her gut. She'd taken note of the changes in her body. "I went to my family doctor and, well…" She opened her mouth, taking in gulp of cool night air.

"I was getting ready to tell you. I had it all figured out. I even had a little gift ready to stuff into your stocking. We got busy with our families. Then I woke up a few days before Christmas and I was bleeding." She stopped talking, and lifted a hand to her face, wiping away a single tear rolling down her cheek. He reached over and clasped her other hand in his. He gave it a gentle squeeze and caressed her skin with his thumb.

"My mom was shocked, but I think she knew what was happening. I didn't. By the time we got to the hospital I had started cramping pretty bad." She wiped away another tear. She'd never said anything about that horrible morning to anyone before now.

"I spent a couple of days in the hospital. Mom and Dad were great. They never pressured me to discuss it or made me feel guilty for not saying anything to them…or for getting pregnant in the first place." She paused again, her breathing a tad ragged.

"That's why you wouldn't see me on Christmas Eve or Christmas Day. Or even the day after. I remembered how pale and sullen you were when we finally exchanged gifts. I just figured you'd had the stomach flu." His head swung around as his gaze sought hers. "Were you still in the hospital for Christmas?"

She shook her head. "I was released mid-afternoon on the twenty-fourth. But I was in no shape to see or talk to anybody." She swallowed a mouthful of guilt. Not even him. Especially him. "They wanted me to call you. When I refused, they encouraged me to talk to somebody, anybody. But I just wanted to be left alone." Her breath hitched.

"Why? Why couldn't you tell *me?*" His speech was raspy.

"Because I blamed myself. I figured I'd done something to cause it. I'd screwed up."

"It wasn't your fault." His voice wobbled.

She fixated on the sand. She couldn't stand to see the betrayal she anticipated would be plain as day on his face, in his eyes. Then and now. They'd created something together and she'd lost it. "I believed it was. We were in our last year of university. I had my part-time job at the paper, and I was trying to land that full-time position. I stressed about exams and the holidays, and being pregnant, Tanner. I had so much going on in my mind, thinking about school, my parents, our future, you. I wasn't sleeping. I wasn't eating right. I figured all that worked against me."

"You can't really believe that."

"At the time, I did. And nobody could convince me otherwise. More importantly, I didn't *want* anybody to try. I was heartbroken. I'd lost my baby. *Our* baby. Hell, it hardly had a chance."

Tanner didn't say a word for about twenty minutes. In the silence of the night, the softness of his voice, when he spoke, made her jolt. "I don't like it, but, I guess I can understand. What I still don't get, though, is why you broke up with me. Even if you had decided never to tell me about the baby, to keep that secret, why end our relationship?"

She shifted to face him straight on, prepared to tell him the rest. Losing the baby was hard. The rest, however, was almost worse. "I didn't want to tie you down with a wife who might not be able to give you children." A sob burned the back of her throat. Tears pooled in her eyes.

"Not give me children? I'm confused."

"The doctor said I'd had a molar pregnancy."

"What does that mean?"

"It's when an incorrect number of chromosomes are transferred to the baby." In a voice as detached as possible, she reiterated what the doctor had told her. Ten years later and she could still hear his exact words. "In a normal pregnancy an equal number of chromosomes are transferred," she explained. "In some cases, the fetus will still develop, but without the proper genetic makeup, it won't survive. I had a baby. Then I didn't. After the miscarriage, they did a D and C—a dilatation and curettage—to confirm the diagnosis and to remove any remaining tissue from my uterus. Apparently, there can be further complications, even the possibility of cancer. I had to go through monthly blood tests and regular ultrasounds for a year to confirm everything was all right, and during that time, I couldn't risk getting pregnant again. Not until my hormone levels were back to normal."

"How are you now?" Concern lay heavy in his question.

"I'm fine. As far as I know anyway."

"What does that mean? Did the doctor tell you that you couldn't have other children?"

"No."

"Can this happen again?"

"The doctor said that it is possible, but the risk of it happening is minimal."

"So if he said the chances are slim, what's the problem?" His snap of frustration came through loud and clear.

"What if I can't have other babies? What if I get pregnant and it happens again? I can't go through that, Tanner, not again." She paused, her voice a bare whisper when she continued. The physical pain and heartbreak a not-so-distant memory. "You'll be a great father someday, Tanner. You deserve a family. I'm just not sure I'm the one who can give it to you."

"Life is full of risks."

"I know." She swallowed, her throat tight. "When I found out I was going to have your baby…God, Tanner…I was so happy. I couldn't wait to tell you."

He reached to put his arm around her, pulling her tight against him.

She snuggled into his side, her relief palpable.

"Even though my parents and the doctor told me everything would be fine, told me it was nothing I did, and not to worry I'd probably have other children, I truly believed I must have done something wrong or my body was in some way defective."

"How did I not notice what you were going through? That you were even pregnant. We were together all the time. Fuck, we went to school together. We lived together."

"Exams kept us pre-occupied for weeks," she said. "I wasn't even showing yet. And then I was at home with my parents and in the hospital. When we got back to the city, you got caught up in the new term and graduation. I didn't say much." She'd used the time back at school to keep her mind busy. She'd cried at night while Tanner studied at the library.

She peeked up to see him fixed on something out across the water. For the second time that that day, tears tracked down his cheeks. She reached a tentative hand up to wipe them away, but stopped halfway there, unsure.

His free hand snagged hers before she reached his face. He lowered their hands to his lap, holding hers tight within his.

Swallowing back her own tears, her voice quivered. "I needed to pretend nothing happened. I know, now, that the likelihood may be slim, but there's still a possibility it could happen again. Back then, I exhibited the classic signs of depression. I let it wrap around me like a blanket, and although intellectually I recognized it for what it was, I couldn't force myself to get the help I needed. Instead, I continued on a downward spiral, until I needed to walk away."

"You should have come to me. I can't believe I didn't notice my girlfriend was going through that. What the fuck kind of guy was I that I didn't notice you hurting?"

"Don't do that to yourself. It wouldn't have mattered. I wasn't ready to talk. I'd started making other plans..."

"What do you mean? What were you doing?"

"I started looking for a place where I could live on my own." His body stiffened.

"I couldn't face hurting you any more than I already had— even if you weren't aware of it. I didn't want to destroy your dreams too. I didn't want to wake up one day to see disappointment in your eyes, or worse, pity. I didn't want you to hate me."

"You could never disappoint me. And I would never hate you." He paused. "I take that back. I'm disappointed that you didn't trust me enough to tell me what was going on with you."

"I've dreamed of having my own children, Tanner, *our* children. All I could think about was you, and what was best for you. I loved you so much, and I knew you loved me, but I couldn't fathom the possibility of you one day turning away from me, angry at not having a complete family. Eventually there would be a huge wall between us. So I decided to set you free."

His voice cracked. "That wasn't your decision to make. You didn't even give me a chance to understand. I didn't want to be free. I wanted you."

She squeezed her eyes shut. God, this sucked. Seeing him in pain sucked. Rehashing all of this now, witnessing his hurt drained her. She didn't want to go through this again. She turned her head and looked out over the water. The light from the moon lit up the surface.

"I loved you more than anything—more than anyone. Even if that were true, that you couldn't have children, it was you I wanted to spend my life with. Surely you know that."

"I didn't know that then, Tanner. We were young. You had your whole life ahead of you."

He dragged in a shaky breath and let it out in slow measured puffs. "If I can only have you in my life, I'll be a happy man."

His use of present tense startled her. A spark of hope bloomed in her chest. She tried to squash it, but it dug in, staking a claim. She had refrained from looking at him. Afraid of what she'd see in his eyes. She focused on the here and now. "I do know better now, but the past is the past, and it still hurts most days. I try not to dwell on it."

"But it's new for me."

"You're right, and I respect that." Regret hung like a weight in the air and in her heart. "I do, but I don't think I can help you through it. In fact, I'd rather not. I'm sorry if that's selfish, but it's taken me all this time to come to grips with what's happened in my life. Work is my life now. Frankly, seeing you this weekend…well, it hasn't been easy. I don't need that pain in my life again. I don't want it in my life. I'm trying to move on." She tried, without success, to keep the wobble out her voice as she rose, and returned to camp.

CHAPTER NINE

DECIDING TO SPEND THE DAY AT THE BEACH, Molly and her friends packed a cooler bursting with a variety of snacks and carried blankets, towels, and a Frisbee. They chatted and chased one another like kids as they walked down the same path she and Tanner had taken the previous night. This time, the beach buzzed with activity when they left the cover of the trees and stepped out onto the sand.

Securing a spot that provided easy access to both sun and shade, they dragged over a picnic table, spread out their blankets and dumped their gear. The men grabbed the Frisbee, heading out to the open sand, but off to the side to avoid running over small children. Once they arranged everything to their satisfaction, Molly and her girlfriends each found some space on the sand, settling in to catch a few rays.

Molly soaked up the warmth of the sun, her body and mind relaxed for the first time in a long time, certainly all weekend.

A shadow fell over her. "Hey, somebody's blocking my sun." When the shadow didn't move, she blinked open her eyes and stared straight into Tanner's sun-bronzed face, his bedroom eyes full of lust.

"I never realized how hot boy-cut shorts are."

She hadn't brought her bikini on this trip, because it was still early in the season, but stretched out on the ground like she was, her tank top dipped low in the cleavage and her hem rode up, exposing her belly. Short shorts finished off the ensemble.

His gaze roved over her body, hunger and desire evident in his hard features. He dropped and stretched out alongside her, resting his head in the palm of his one hand while he used the other to sprinkle a handful of sand up her body slowly. The small grains bounced around on her flesh.

"Interested in joining me for a stroll through the woods? We could check out the spot with the big boulders we visited yesterday. Or, maybe we could slip back to the tents and find something to occupy us while everyone's here at the beach."

She chuckled, smothering a sigh of relief that he didn't appear angry. "You just want to ditch our friends and go have sex."

"I'm sure they'd understand." She imagined the swirls of grey in his eyes behind his sunglasses. His cocky grin on his face made her relax and laugh harder. God, it felt great to laugh.

"Maybe I just want to talk. I haven't talked to you in a long time." A part of her teased, but the other part had missed being able to talk to him for the past ten years.

"We talked just last night."

"You know what I mean."

He huffed. "We could. I suppose. But what I had in mind would be more fun." His eyebrows wiggled above those dark shades and he snaked a fingertip from knee to hip and then up her side. She jerked when he touched on a ticklish spot.

Of course it would be. Unfortunately, it would also make her fall for him again, and she couldn't risk that. Sleeping with one another would not help the situation and would only create more heartache when she went home tomorrow—alone. "I don't think that's a good idea. The weekend's almost over. You'll have your restaurant deal to work out, and I'll have…" What would she have? Oh, yeah, her job.

"Molly—"

"Come on you two, girls against the boys." Colleen jumped up, slapping Tanner in the back of the head as she jumped over their prone bodies on her way to join the others at the makeshift beach volleyball court.

For the remainder of the day, Molly managed to avoid intimate moments with Tanner as they played volleyball with their friends, occasionally stopping to rehydrate or to switch out players with fellow campers who asked to join. A couple of the guys braved the cold water and then came out shivering, wearing wicked grins and looking for the nearest female to cozy up to.

When the sun began its descent, they packed their stuff and walked single file back to the campsite. Their eyes sparkled in their tired, sunburned faces. Molly had been exchanging meaningful glances with Tanner the whole afternoon. His looks said *let's get down and dirty.* Hers said *I'd love to, but it's time to move on.* She gave him kudos for his tenacity, though.

She thrived on the familiar feelings of being around him again, but she needed to shore up her reserves for the good-bye to come.

* * *

Matt and Sam volunteered to cook, so while they prepared the evening meal, the others jumped in the showers.

Soon, supper was over, the sun long gone, and backlit by moonlight, dark clouds sailed through the sky, pushed by the wind. A low rumble of thunder rolled through the night, and lightning flashed in the distant sky.

Tanner's chest expanded as he inhaled, the smell of rain permeating the air. A storm brewed in his body too.

He closed his eyes, remembering the sight of Molly lying on the beach earlier. Desire coursed through his blood, heating it to near combustible levels. If only they'd been alone. In his mind, he'd stretched out over her, pressed his chest to hers, settled between her soft thighs and plunged deep and hard into her hot, tight body, right there on the sand, under the sun.

He shook his head and groaned, shifting to lean forward, hiding his condition as he struggled to get his body under control. The afternoon activities had kept his libido in check, but it didn't extinguish his lust by any stretch. His skin tingled and his body hummed, aggravated by the energy in the air and by her attempts to stay clear of him.

His friends sat around the fire, engaged in quiet conversations. They waited for the rain to start in earnest, knowing it would restrict them to their tents when it came.

Tanner bided his time. This was his last opportunity. He had to make it count.

"So, Tanner." Brad's question interrupted his internal planning. "When do you start work in the city?"

With herculean effort, he turned his focus to the conversation. "I still need to finalize the deal, but if all goes well, I plan to officially open the restaurant in November. I originally wanted to open in time for Thanksgiving, but I have to complete some renovations first. I also have to make a quick trip back to BC to tie up a few loose ends there."

"Do you have a theme for the place?"

"I have an idea, nothing concrete though. All I can say right now is that it won't be a pub, and it won't be too exclusive. I also have a line on a great chef. A friend of mine from BC is looking for a change. I'm hoping I can work something out with him."

Violet laughed. "That doesn't give us much to go on, Tanner."

"Sorry. I don't want to say much until the plans are completed and the deal is done. I can say you won't be disappointed. The food will be top quality for a reasonable price."

"So what will you do between now and opening?" Matt piped into the conversation.

"I need to spend some time with my parents, and I want to relax while I can. I figure I'll be around here for most of June and July, with trips into Ottawa, of course." Tanner swung his head to watch for any reaction from Molly. "If I'm going to stay, I'll need to find a place to live."

Her eyes widened, and her pupils darkened.

Pleased, he switched his attention back to Brad, but a smile fought for freedom. "We'll have to spend more time together, bud."

"Absolutely. I'm glad you're back, man. Maybe we can plan a few more camping trips before the end of the season."

"I'd like that."

They continued to chat about plans for the upcoming summer until the first spatters of rain fell. It didn't take long before the drops became steady. When the fire began to hiss and spit, it was time to call it a night.

Tanner made a quick grab for Molly's hand when she walked by him. "Come with me."

Her gaze flicked over his face and settled on his eyes. She squinted, as though searching for something. Indecision seemed to do battle in hers, but she nodded.

He led her over to Brad's car, opened the back passenger door and ushered her inside, closing the door with a soft click behind him. The heavens accepted that as their cue, and buckets of rain plastered the roof and windshield, obliterating the view of everything outside the car.

CHAPTER TEN

U NCONCERNED WITH THE RAIN POUNDING DOWN around them, he turned to Molly and without a word cradled her face in his hands. He leaned in and brushed his lips against hers, pouring every molecule of his being into that simple kiss. He licked and nibbled his way across her top lip and then moved to her bottom one before seeking entrance to the delight he knew lay beyond. When she opened her mouth in a gasp, he took it as an invitation. They seduced each other with their tongues, dancing to a song so beautiful; he believed he heard actual music in his head.

He lured her in close, deepening the connection. In his mind, a litany of past, present, and future moments played out to some melody for his ear alone. He withdrew from her mouth and stared down into her face, longing to share the fantasies he envisioned of their future together. The emotions reflected in hers made his heart stutter. He saw tenderness, hope, and—he prayed—maybe love?

"Tanner?"

"Shhh."

Wrapped in darkness, they rediscovered one another by touch. With gentle reverence, they undressed each other, one piece of clothing at a time, stopping along the way to explore and to place soft kisses and tender licks on the other's body as each area became exposed. Every now and again, a flash of lightning provided a spark of light. The inside of the car filled with throaty moans and groaned sighs.

"It feels like we're the only two people in the world."

He couldn't agree more.

Rain beat down on their shelter, and thunder rumbled overhead. The car swayed. Was that the wind or was that them?

He didn't know.

He didn't care.

When Molly reached between his legs and cradled his cock in her soft grip, he closed his eyes. Fuck.

"You're so hard."

"And really sensitive, so if you don't want me to go off in your hand, you need to be careful."

Her fingers traveled up and down in a teasing caress, rubbing her thumb over the engorged head on each upward stroke. Fluid eased from the slit. She wiped it away, lifted her thumb to her mouth, and licked it clean. She shifted, finding a position that allowed her to cant her upper body over his lap. Her tongue swept a path along the length of his shaft.

Oh, Lord.

He growled low in his throat and wrapped his fingers in her hair, wanting to guide her with subtle pressure, but not wanting to hurry the show. When moonlight escaped the clouds, he caught glimpses of her swallowing his cock an inch at a time. It was the hottest fucking thing ever.

Molly moved up and down, her mouth warm and wet. Her right hand fisted the bottom half, working in tandem with each bob of her head. Come boiled in his balls, the urge to fill that hot, delectable little orifice, strangled him. "That's so fucking hot, Molly, but you gotta stop. You're killing me."

Oh, but he'd die a happy man. He gritted his teeth, fighting to restrain the bone-deep desire to fuck her mouth. She retreated, but just to tease him with a wicked grin.

Then the little witch started licking him with long, sure strokes, wrapping her lips around the aching head, applying the smallest bit of suction each time she reached the top. She drove him nuts, taking him deeper into the warm recess of her mouth on each downward stroke until she no longer licked him, but swallowed him whole.

The tip of his cock bumped the back of her throat. He squeezed his eyes shut.

"Sweet Jesus. I can't take much more. Stop. Please." He gave her hair a hard tug, pulling her away, drawing out a sharp cry of disappointment.

She glanced up, her eyes dark and slumberous, her lips slick and puffy.

Sitting amid the darkness surrounding the car, a visceral sense of male possessiveness hit him hard in the gut. He pushed her back against the car's door, lifting her one leg to rest over the back seat, the other over the front. With her spread wide open, he waited a beat for a flash of lightning to offer him a view of her sweet, succulent pussy.

God must have been listening. A deep rumble shook the ground and thunder rolled around them, rocking the vehicle, as a brilliant flash lit up the interior. The smell of electricity charged the air, intermingled with the fragrance of her arousal. The light lasted only a second, but it was long enough to imprint on his brain the sight of her, spread open, ripe and ready for his taking. Her eyes were round, her lips parted, and her pussy lush, swollen, and moist.

"Oh, Molly, honey, you look so pretty." He shoved his hands under the cheeks of her ass, raising her toward his eager mouth. He bent down to swipe his tongue along her velvet-soft lips, licking the juice already dripping free. "Mmm."

Her body trembled, and she uttered a throaty groan. She jerked her hips, bringing her closer.

He would have preferred to take his time, but one taste of her honey had him hooked. He delved in and ate her with gusto, plunging his tongue deep inside, groaning when the walls of her pussy sucked him deeper.

He snacked on her, tasted every morsel she offered. His tongue toyed with her clit, flicking back and forth over it before sucking the swollen nub into his mouth.

Violent shudders rolled through her body. Whimpers of frustration fell from her lips, and she grabbed a fistful of his hair and pressed tight against his face, seeking release from the torture he so lovingly dished out.

He chuckled, the sound coming from deep in his throat. "Come for me. I want to feel your juices coat my tongue."

"Oh, God, it feels…I don't want you to stop, Tanner. Please, please, don't stop." Her breathing was ragged, her voice hoarse.

"Oh, I'm not stopping. Not until you come. I want to taste you."

She growled like a large cat. He smiled, thrilled that his blunt language seemed to turn her on.

He tipped her ass forward a little more, watching with avid

fascination when some of her cream slid from her opening and trickled down to her puckered rear. He followed the stream with his tongue, rimming her ass. She gasped and jolted, but didn't complain. Could this be a new sensation for her? Anal play was not something they had indulged in before. Curious, he dipped a finger into her pussy, driving it in and out a few times, until it was nice and slick. He used the moisture to massage her back entrance, applying steady pressure as he did.

Intent on what he was doing, he almost missed the fact that she'd gone still.

He dared a glance to gauge her reaction.

Her focus stayed riveted on what he was doing, her eyes wide, her pupils large and dark. She seemed to be holding her breath.

He dropped his gaze back down, and the sky lit up again as he slid his finger into her ass, mesmerized as he watched it sink past the second knuckle.

Her gasp brought his attention back to her face, fearful he'd hurt her. Captivated, he watched her eyes roll back and her jaw drop open, her expression one of unadulterated pleasure.

He eased his finger out, then drilled it back in again. She reached with her hips to meet him halfway. He put his tongue back to her clit, laving her slit while he finger-fucked her ass.

She began to pant, thrusting her hips in time with his movements. Shivers raced along her body, making his fingers tingle where they made contact with her skin.

"Oh. My. God." Her words escaped as a cry.

Faster and faster, they moved in a synchronized dance.

A clap of thunder drowned out the groan rising through her. She thrashed against him, begging him for more, until finally, she bowed her body, arching away from his touch, and a strangled keening sound was ripped from her throat. She exploded, her come spilling out to coat his hand.

Slipping his finger out from the tightness of her ass, he grasped her hips and licked her sex through the throes of her climax.

Little by little, her body began to relax, and her breathing returned to near normal.

His body continued to thrum, impatient for release. He relaxed his grip and retrieved a condom. His hands shook. He sat up and pulled her astride his lap. He had never been so fucking turned on. This woman sucked the breath right out of him. He couldn't wait to feel her wet heat surrounding his throbbing cock.

Biceps bulging, he lifted her over his straining erection and slowly lowered her onto his shaft. His jaw clenched tight, his muscles straining as he fought the impulse to ram into her.

When he was finally sheathed in her tight channel, he stilled and drew in a lungful of air, desperate to gain control over his intoxicating need to pound into her. She wriggled around him.

"Fuck." He grasped her hips and began moving her up and down the length of his cock. "You're so freaking hot." The glove-tight sensation of gliding the flesh on his cock back and forth against the smooth walls of her vagina sent ripples of pleasure running through his body. Hot, slippery fluid warmed his dick. He rocked his body into hers, grinding his groin against her pelvis, pressing to fit himself as deep as he could get.

"Oh, my, I'm going to come again. Go faster."

"Oh, yeah, honey. I can do faster." His arms trembled as he shifted her up and down on his lap. Sweat dripped from his brow. The smack of her ass hitting his thighs was erotic as hell. He muttered between clenched teeth. "I don't think I can. I can't hold on, Molly. You feel...tight and so fucking hot."

She moaned deep and guttural in the hot, closed-in space. Her breaths came in hard pants. She raised her hands to her nipples.

The sight of her pinching and pulling her pert tits kicked his craving up another notch. He growled like an animal. Swooping forward, he nudged her hands away with his chin and licked and sucked at each breast. Moving between the two, he rocked his hips faster.

"Tanner."

"I'm almost there, honey. Just...another...minute."

Then she put her hands on his chest, tugging at *his* nipples. The sensation stunned him. He let her breast fall from his mouth and threw his head back against the headrest, his jaw slack. Ah, man. His balls and spine tingled. His cock was hard as steel inside her, ready to detonate.

The pressure began to build, spiraling tight. Seconds from blowing, he somehow managed to increase the pace, thrusting deep as she rode him hard, searching for that sweet spot. She reached behind her, arched her chest, and cupped his sac in her hand, closing her fingers around him. She tugged and squeezed with just the right amount of pressure.

Lightning flashed.

Thunder crashed.

She screamed and he roared as he erupted. His body jerked as he held her in a bruising grip and drove his cock home one last time, stopping when he bottomed out.

With a long, throaty groan, spasm after spasm ripped through his core. How could so much fluid come from one man?

He slumped back against the seat of the car, drained, sated, and euphoric.

How in God's name could he ever live his life without this woman in his bed, by his side, sharing the good times—and the not-so-great times?

* * *

Molly collapsed against Tanner's chest, both working to get their breathing under control. His heart kept time with hers. Holy shit. Sex, even with Tanner, had never been this intense.

She lifted her head, but had to will her arm to lift so she could clear a small area of condensation off the glass. The storm had stopped, and a gentle rain fell now. The fogged-over windows would ensure their retreat remained private for a while longer yet.

He cascaded his hand over her hair and stroked down her bare back. "Wow." His voice was deeper than normal, husky, sexy.

"Yeah." Her heart blossomed with full-blown love. Wild fantasies of a happy ever after flashed through her head. She had decided long ago that she wouldn't find love again. Not like she'd experienced with him all those years ago.

After seeing him again, making love with him, baring her pain to him, she wondered if it was possible for her to be with him again. Could she take the risk? Did he even want her?

She reflected over the weekend, remembering the tender glances, the soft-spoken words, the gentle touches.

While her internal struggle continued, he caressed her back with soft lazy strokes. She sighed and settled against him, her arms reaching to loop around his neck. She lifted her head to gaze into his eyes. Excitement mingled with hope at what she believed she saw staring back at her.

He leaned in and kissed her. "I've never stopped loving you, Molly. I thought I had, but I'd only been fooling myself. I figured it out about six months ago."

"But—"

"I want you back. I don't want to pick up where we left off. I want to start over. I want to get to know the beautiful, sexy woman you are today. I want us to have a life together."

When she opened her mouth, he placed a finger against her lips. "Just listen. I want you in my life. It's the reason I came home. It's the reason I'm buying the restaurant. I can make you happy, Molly, I promise. If we're fortunate enough to have children, that would be wonderful. And if not, well, there *are* other ways." He stopped, but she waited, sensing he had more to say.

"I spent the last ten years separated from you. Part of that time, I was angry. After a while, I discovered I was more hurt than angry. I didn't understand then, but I do now, at least some of it. I've never found another woman who even came close to being somebody I wanted to share my life with every day. Please, give us a chance." His eyes shimmered with pent-up emotion.

"I love you too, Tanner. I don't know if I'll have problems with getting pregnant or the pregnancy itself, but I do know that I want to be with you, regardless of whether we can have a child of our own or not." She paused. "I was too scared then. Too scared to keep you and have you end up so disappointed in me." She took a deep breath. "I'm still scared, but I'm willing to try. I think you're worth the risk."

He enclosed her in his arms. Molly laid her head against his chest and released the breath she'd been holding for what felt like forever. Savoring the moment, they lay wrapped together, basking in the afterglow, while she listened to the light patter of rain on the roof.

In the wee hours, he made love to her again, this time unhurried, but no less powerful.

CHAPTER ELEVEN

MOLLY HATED SAYING GOOD-BYE TO HER FRIENDS. Although most of them lived within driving distance, they didn't get together often enough. Breakfast was a relaxed, quiet affair. She sat with Tanner at one end of the picnic table. At her age, it was hard to believe shyness still existed, but she found herself casting quick peeks in his direction, somewhat fearful that the previous night had been a dream.

When his glance swung to meet hers, the emotions displayed on his face and the hungry heat in his eyes left her mouth dry and her heart thumping double-time. His arm snaked around behind her to rest against her lower back, before moving to caress up and down her spine. He seemed happy and content—a man in love.

They spent the remainder of the morning dismantling tents, packing clothes and bedding, storing food, and clearing the site of waste. Molly multitasked, using the time to replay the events of the past few days in her mind. In less than four days, she had fallen in love.

Or had she every really fallen *out* of love?

So much had changed. Tanner was home, and he wanted her back. The guilt she had been living with for the past ten years didn't run so deep anymore. Older, wiser now, she discovered that with the right person at her side, she could be strong enough to take any risk, because that person loved her enough to share it with her.

She gazed over to where he stood by the cars joking with the other men. He glanced up, and curved his lips into a slow smile. The warm feeling that filled her almost made her dizzy. At the end of the day, right or wrong, the past was the past and with a shared history, and a shared pain, they at least didn't need to start from scratch. She could move forward from here.

Colleen drew Molly aside, her eyes wide with curiosity. "What's going on between you and Tanner?"

"Nothing. Why?"

Colleen narrowed her eyes and scrunched her forehead. "Don't give me that innocent crap. You're my best friend. I know you. Something's up. Spill."

"Um…I don't really want to talk about it right now or right here."

"Why not?"

Molly widened her eyes.

"You guys had sex, didn't you?"

She dropped her gaze down to the chipped polish on her toes.

"Let me see your face."

Molly raised her head.

Colleen let out a tiny squeal. "When?"

She offered a teasing grin. "The first time or the last time?"

"Oh, my God!" This time, her shriek captured the interest of their other friends.

"Can you keep it down please? You're attracting attention."

"Details."

"Not here. Besides, I want to keep things low-key for a while." She kicked at a stone. "At least until we know where this relationship is going, until it's more stable."

Serious now, Colleen studied her. "I can understand that. Are you good though, honey?"

"Yeah, I'm very good."

"What happened back then? It's been ten years. What happened then? What happened now?"

"This really isn't the place for me to go into the details. But I will tell you. I promise."

"Fair enough. What about what happened this weekend, between you and Tanner?"

"Let's just say we've discussed the issues that separated us long ago and want to see where things can go from here."

"Was the sex hot? Can you tell me that at least?" Colleen had a wicked gleam in her eye.

Molly fanned herself.

"Oh, we so have to schedule a girls' afternoon—real soon."

Molly chuckled. "Tanner still has to finalize the restaurant deal. While that happens, he'll be going back and forth between his parents place and mine. But don't worry. I'll make sure I keep my schedule open for you too."

Colleen had tears in her eyes and a smile on her face. "I'm happy for you." She gave her a long, tight hug before moving away to finish packing.

Long before the others had started the day, Tanner and Molly, cuddled in the back seat of the car, had discussed plans for the summer, striving to work those plans around their budding relationship. He planned to go back to town with

Brad and spend a few days with his parents, but promised to drive to Ottawa to see her the following weekend.

She would have to settle for some heated phone sex until then. She'd never had phone sex before, but the concept thrilled her.

Both agreed to take their time. They wanted to do this right.

Molly strolled over to join the others standing by the cars.

"It sure was a surprise to see you this weekend." Violet placed a hand on Tanner's shoulder. Turning to see Molly approach, she grinned. "A nice surprise, I believe."

Tanner shifted his stance when Molly come up beside him, hooked an arm around her waist and hugged her close, treating her to a special smile. "I couldn't agree more."

Brad studied them for a moment and grinned. "Hey, man, looks like we have some catching up to do on the ride back to town." She felt her cheeks heat as Tanner gave her a squeeze.

"Let us know if you need some help with the renos." Matt was stuffing a cooler into the back of his SUV. "And don't forget to invite us to your opening."

Tanner chuckled. "You can expect personal invites. Once I finalize my plans, I'll let you know how you can help, and we'll set up a private event to celebrate. Dinner will be on me." He moved away from Molly and walked over to give Sam a pat on the back before he pulled Olivia into his arms. "Congrats again. You're going to make wonderful parents."

Time to leave.

With a few tears, Molly wished them well and backed away to stand beside Tanner and Brad as the others drove away in their respective cars, waving until they disappeared around the bend.

Brad hugged Molly and then climbed into his car.

Tanner swiveled to face her. He hauled her close and pressed his lips to hers. "I can't wait to see you again. It's going to be a very long week."

She leaned into him. "It's four days. I'm sure you want to spend some time with your parents. Count yourself lucky if you manage to get away on Friday."

"Oh, don't worry about that. I will be in your apartment by dinnertime. Wear something special for my arrival." He winked.

"How about heels?"

"Just heels?"

"You'll have to wait and see." She felt alive, ready to take on anything the future tossed her way.

With a growl, he gave her a final hug and a deep, searing kiss that singed her lips.

"Get in your car before I change my mind about visiting my parents. Brad and I will follow you out of the park."

She hesitated, looking down at his chest rather than in his face. "Tanner?"

"Yeah."

"I'm glad you came back, and I'm glad you don't hate me. I can't begin to tell you how much I've missed you." The last came out on a near sob.

"I know. I missed you too, sweetheart. We'll take it one step at a time." He smiled, and inclined his head in for yet one more heated embrace. "I'm looking forward to playing house with you this summer."

She laughed, swatted his ass, and gave him one last quick smooch. Then she ran to her car and jumped in before she changed *her* mind about him visiting his parents.

The trip home was the opposite from her drive to the park on Friday. Instead of visits down memory lane, she dreamed of bright possibilities ahead.

Caught up in blissful happiness, she sang along with the radio on the way home, her smile honest and true for the first time in years.

EPILOGUE

Five Years Later

"COME ON, MOLLY, WE NEED TO GET ON THE ROAD. I'd like to be there before the burgers are cold and beer is warm." Tanner's favorite pastime these days—teasing his slow-moving wife. She ambled over, her smile radiant, her hands hugging her swollen belly. Pregnant with their second child, she remained the most stunning woman he had ever laid eyes on, and he loved her more each day.

Their daughter, Ava, clinging to the hem of Molly's blouse, toddled along beside her.

"*I'm* ready to go. I was waiting for your daughter to take a final potty break before we put her in the car. It's a long drive to the park for a two-year-old."

He laughed.

Ava released her hold on Molly and ran toward him, her chubby little legs churning and sporting an ear-to-ear grin. Her eyes went big and round as she pulled her arms back, elbows pointed, hands curled into tiny fists. He was familiar with that look and recognized the signs.

Tanner bent down low, ready to catch her. Ava came in at full tilt, leaping as only a spirited two-year-old could. In one fluid motion, he grabbed his daughter around the waist and stood, swinging her high in the air, eliciting screams of little-girl pleasure, before he turned to settle her into the car seat, and buckle her in. Leaning inside the vehicle, he kissed her on the forehead. She rewarded him with a pat on the cheek. She giggled with delight when he closed the door and then pressed his face against the glass.

Molly got in and secured her own seat belt. He gave his wife a resounding smooch on the lips before closing her car door and then walking around to climb in on the driver's side.

"Go park, Daddy, go park." Ava clapped her little hands, thrilled to go on an adventure.

They were off for their annual May Two-Four weekend. Now, however, it was more of a family get-together. Sam and Olivia would be there with their twins, as would Colleen and Steve, who married not long after Ava's birth. They lived in Ottawa now—eagerly expecting their first child in the fall.

Brad and his new wife would be there too, and Matt and Violet, who eventually hooked up—to the surprise of everyone but Molly. Wedding bells were in the future for those two. Seeing his friends happy and settled in their lives went a long way in making up for the time he lost with them.

With the help of a therapist, he and Molly had worked through their past. He had spent time discussing his feelings about the pregnancy and baby, and a sense of loss for something he had known nothing about.

Thankfully, Molly's other pregnancies had been normal, though with each, they'd been on pins and needles for the first few months.

After six months of renovations and then decorating, they'd opened their restaurant, and even with a small handful of hiccups, it had turned into a wise and successful business venture. So much so, he'd begun looking for a second location.

WORTH THE RISK

Tanner glanced in the rear-view mirror, amazed as he always was when he looked at his tiny Ava.

"Tanner?" Molly speared him a curious look. "Everything alright?"

He smiled. He had a gorgeous wife, a beautiful daughter and another baby on the way. He nodded. "Everything's good."

Life was better than good.

He and Molly had found their way back to each other, proving in life, and in love, some risks were worth taking.

ABOUT THE AUTHOR

Shoes are her addiction, but books are her passion. Anne reads many genres of romance, but prefers to write sexy stories with a side of those sinful pleasures your mom never told you about—along with a happy ending, of course.

Anne juggles a full time job and a family. She's a Canadian author who lives in Eastern Ontario with her wonderfully supportive husband, three awesome kids, Rocky the bearded dragon, and Lily the chocolate lab.

Discover more about Anne Lange here:

Website
http://authorannelange.com/

Facebook
http://www.facebook.com/AuthorAnneLange

Twitter: @Anne_Lange
http://twitter.com/Anne_Lange

Goodreads
http://www.goodreads.com/author/show/6896566.Anne_Lange

Newsletter
http://authorannelange.com/newsletter/

Email
Anne_Lange66@yahoo.ca

CHECK OUT THE FIRST BOOKS IN ANNE'S OTHER SERIES

FRIENDS WITH BENEFITS
THE VAULT SERIES

Can sexual exploration lead to three times the bliss?

Tyler had no idea his wife Angela's desires so closely matched his own. But when some unguarded pillow talk reveals her fantasy of two men at once, Tyler jumps at the chance to make her happy.

Enlisting the help of his best friend Connor, who'd shared some threesome adventures with him in the past, Tyler secretly hopes exploring Angela's fantasies will lead to his own personal desire—a permanent threesome with the two people he loves most in the world.

Connor can't believe it when his best friend asks him to seduce his wife. Then he meets Angela, and all the women in his past fade away. With Tyler's blessing, Connor sets out to melt Angela's reserve, and when Tyler joins the party, the three of them set the sheets on fire.

Angela is floored when her husband suggests they explore some of her fantasies—things she'd only read about but never in a million years thought she'd actually do. Sandwiched between Tyler and Connor, she's never felt so treasured, so protected, so loved.

But the reality proves much more complicated than the fantasy. She loves her husband, but she finds herself falling for his best friend too. That's not normal, is it? What will people think?

SLIDING INTO HOME
A NEW LEAGUE SERIES

Can an injured ex ball player convince the woman he wakes up married to in Las Vegas to take a second chance on him?

After spending the last four months drowning his sorrows over the end of his baseball career, Jack Bishop finds himself winging through the blue skies to Las Vegas, not so ready to spend the weekend with some woman his best friend set him up with. He expects a paid escort. What he gets is the woman he walked away from ten years ago to pursue his passion, and she's not very happy to see him.

Devyn Tate believes she's quite capable of finding somebody to take her out to dinner. She's no longer looking for a lifelong promise. She has a commitment only to her battery-operated toy to fulfill that particular need. Yet her friends have managed to talk her into spending the weekend in Las Vegas, on a blind date of all things. They promise the guy is trustworthy. They insist that she should have fun. Unfortunately, fun is not what she envisions when she discovers Jack Bishop lying on the floor of her suite in nothing but his underwear that's on backward, and she has a wedding ring on her finger

HER CHOICE
FAMILY TIES, BOOK 1

He's not her father's pick. But he's her only option.

Gage Barrett's goal is to bring one of the biggest crime bosses in the city to his knees. The man runs drugs, extorts money, and has the profits laundered by the pretty Angelena's father. Gage just has to get close enough to find the evidence he needs to put the guy away for good before another family is forced to live through a pain Gage is all too familiar with.

Angelena Bianco doesn't understand why her father is so insistent she marry the son of one of his clients. Santo is a thug and she wants nothing to do with him. It will be a cold day in hell before she'll walk down any aisle to that man. When the day comes for her to get married, it will be to a man of her choosing, not her father's.

Lena has two months and few options. She needs to find a husband, fast before she's forced into a situation she can't live with.

FOREVER STARTS TODAY
THE FOREVER SERIES

Love doesn't last, not even in Forever.

Sadie has been disappointed time and again and gives no credence to the myth she'll one day find her true love. Her small hometown offers little in the way of opportunity, excitement, or anonymity, but guilt and resentment keep her Forever bound.

Asher craves distance from the city and the business his father insists he join. He's hoping the quaint town of Forever will spark his muse and give him clarity to make major life decisions. He's not looking for love, but a strange encounter and an odd gift give him a glimpse into a future where his destiny becomes clearer every day.

Available April 2017!

FREE SHORT STORY

Don't forget to get your FREE copy of Game Night, a sinfully short and erotic story by Anne.

http://dl.bookfunnel.com/eysouov4fz

It's time to play.

A photographer who likes to play games entices a professional ball player into spending the evening in front of her camera – naked.

CHECK YOUR INHIBITIONS
AT THE DOOR. . .

WWW.AUTHORANNELANGE.COM

hotRom publishing